My name is Callum Ormond.
I am fifteen
and I am a hunted fugitive . . .

CONSPIRACY 365

BOOK FIVE: MAY

Scholastic $9.50

To Alice, Charlie and Lily

Scholastic Australia
345 Pacific Highway
Lindfield NSW 2070
An imprint of Scholastic Australia Pty Limited
(ABN 11 000 614 577)
PO Box 579
Gosford NSW 2250
www.scholastic.com.au

Part of the Scholastic Group
Sydney • Auckland • New York • Toronto • London • Mexico City
• New Delhi • Hong Kong • Buenos Aires • Puerto Rico

First published by Scholastic Australia in 2010.
Text copyright © Gabrielle Lord, 2010.
Illustrations copyright © Scholastic Australia, 2010.
Graphics by Nicole Leary.
Cover copyright © Scholastic Australia, 2010.
Cover design by Natalie Winter.
Cover photography: running male by Wendell Teodoro © Scholastic
Australia, 2010; close-up of boy's face by Michael Bagnall ©
Scholastic Australia, 2010; house on fire © Pyastolova Nadya/
Shutterstock; stormy sky © Adisa/Shutterstock; jet and cloudy sky
© istockphoto.com/Achim Prill.
Internal photography: paper on page 067 © istockphoto.com/Luseen
Heinlein; paper on page 045 © istockphoto.com/Royce DeGrie.

National Library of Australia Cataloguing-in-Publication entry:
Lord, Gabrielle, 1946-
  Conspiracy 365: May / Gabrielle Lord.
  ISBN 978-1-74169-037-8 (pbk.)
A823.3

Printed by McPherson's Printing Group, Maryborough, Victoria.

Scholastic Australia's policy, in association with McPherson's Printing Group,
is to use papers that are renewable and made efficiently from wood grown in
sustainable forests, so as to minimise its environmental footprint.

10 9 8 7 6 5 4 3 2 1   10 11 12 13 14 / 0

CONSPIRACY 365

BOOK FIVE: MAY

GABRIELLE LORD

SCHOLASTIC
SYDNEY AUCKLAND NEW YORK TORONTO LONDON MEXICO CITY
NEW DELHI HONG KONG BUENOS AIRES PUERTO RICO

PREVIOUSLY . . .

1 APRIL

A cop, who doesn't realise who I am, comes running down to our high-speed crash site. He takes over holding Lachlan's head out of the water, while I disappear into the bush. Sumo and Kelvin track me down, but their chase is interrupted by gunshots—the three of us are caught in the crossfire of an army drill!

Sumo's taken down by a bullet, but I make it out of there and finally call Boges. He tells me Gabbi's life support is being switched off— I have one week to get back to the city and do whatever I can to save her life. A quick decision to try and steal a ride from an old lady called Melba Snipe—by jumping into the boot of her car—leads to a surprising encounter.

3 APRIL

Runaway Griff Kirby and I meet and decide to make our way to the city together.

4 APRIL

I find out from Boges that Gabbi's life support is being turned off early! I rush to the hospital and sneak through to the Intensive Care Unit, just in time to see her. She looks fragile and helpless lying there in a coma, but when I start talking her eyelids begin to flutter—it's enough of a sign of improvement for the doctors to keep her alive! Rafe tries to stop Mum from hitting the emergency buzzer when she sees me . . . I'm shattered to witness the fear in my mum's face. She still thinks I'm a monster.

5 APRIL

I discover a little boathouse on the riverbank at Greenaway Park—a perfect new hideout.

19 APRIL

I'm desperate to see Boges, but he's paranoid about being followed. I talk him through the Ormond Riddle over the phone.

23 APRIL

I see my double coming out of the local high school.

25 APRIL

Rafe and I run into each other at the cenotaph.

He quickly pulls out his phone, so I take off. He shouts after me, bringing unwanted attention—people begin recognising me! Fearing I'll be caught, I seek refuge at Repro's.

29 APRIL
Boges and Winter finally come to see me at the boathouse. I show them the Riddle, but before long an argument breaks out and Winter leaves. Sligo's thugs turn up, forcing us both to flee. I go after Winter and find her at the cenotaph. She tells me Kelvin has tipped off Sligo on my location. Where's he getting that information from? When I return to the boathouse, I find it's been trashed and the stuff from my backpack's missing. Someone grabs me from behind and I feel a piercing pain in my neck. Everything blacks out.

30 APRIL
I wake up in Leechwood Lodge Asylum! Someone's locked me up in the nuthouse, and stripped me of my identity! I've lost everything. How am I going to get out?!

1 MAY

245 days to go . . .

Leechwood Lodge Asylum

7:07 am

The sound of screaming woke me up with a violent jolt. My hazy nightmare with the white toy dog and the crying baby had blended in with the very real, desperate cries of the people in this place. My dazed confusion lasted only a second before I accepted the equally horrible reality: that I'd been kidnapped and locked up in Leechwood Lodge, a psychiatric institution, inhabited by homicidal maniacs, the mentally insane—and now me.

Just days ago I was hiding out in the quiet little boathouse on the water, slowly making progress and actually getting somewhere, and now I was in this high-security psych ward, under a false identity, and everything was lost.

7:10 am

There was no point in pounding on the door or joining in with the screaming out for help—the orderlies had made that very clear.

I flopped back on the yellowing pillow. Leechwood was the perfect name for this place: it seemed to suck the life out of you. My mood was as heavy as lead as I thought about what had happened to me in the last few days.

Vulkan Sligo had stolen my dad's drawings and the copy of the Ormond Riddle—thanks to the treacherous Winter Frey, who must have tipped him off about my Greenaway Park boathouse hideout. Or had she? I'd been so angry with her earlier, but I was no longer sure why. She had seemed pretty determined to protect me from the black Subaru when it showed up at Memorial Park, to stop whoever was in it from coming for me. She put herself on the line to distract them and get them off my trail . . . but then someone trashed the boathouse and grabbed me anyway.

A sick taste filled my mouth as I thought of all the things I'd worked so hard to discover and decipher that were now gone. The past four months of hell had all been for nothing! Everything I'd uncovered, while having to live on the streets and be constantly on the run, had been served on a silver platter to Vulkan Sligo or Oriana de la Force, or whoever was responsible for trapping me in this place. Dad's drawings and the Ormond Riddle were gone. I had done all that work only to help those thieves!

Locked in here I was useless—I couldn't do anything about it. I rolled over and buried my face in the pillow. Everything hurt. My neck ached from the tranquilliser dart, which seemed to have also done something to flare up the dull pain in my right shoulder again. At least I wasn't in the straitjacket anymore—one of the orderlies removed it during the night when I had to go to the bathroom, warning me that if I wasn't on my best behaviour, it would go right back on again.

I didn't want to be here—I didn't want to be who I was—it was all too hard. I wished I could just go home and be with Mum and Gabbi, so we could learn to be a family again. We needed a chance to get used to the idea of Dad being gone. Why did it have to be like this?

The screams were suddenly taken over by an ominous silence. I sat up, my feet hanging down, skimming the cold floor. I was miserable and it wasn't just being locked up in this place that was doing it. I'd had a fight with Boges, my best friend, and I couldn't blame him if he just gave up on me. I had no idea about Winter. I felt I didn't have a friend in the world. Mum thought I was nuts and Uncle Rafe was too caught up worrying about the estate and the practical side of things. The only glimmer of hope right now was Gabbi. I knew she'd be behind me. Instinctively, my fingers went to twist the Celtic ring she'd given me, but of course it was no longer there. I'd slipped it on her finger at the hospital. The thought of her eyelids flickering and her gradual recovery was the only good thing that had come out of the last four months.

And now this.

How was I going to get out?

7:17 am

The screaming started up again, closer than before.

'I'll kill him!' a man's voice shrieked. 'He's an impostor! A replacement! I'll kill him! Where is he? Where is the real Dr Snudgeglasser?'

Footsteps pounded down the corridor. Heavy doors opened and closed with urgency. I had the sense that the staff at the asylum were racing around the place trying to control someone.

The voice of whoever wanted to kill Dr Snudgeglasser was muffled, then fell silent once more.

Dr Snudgeglasser's name was on my chart as being my psychiatrist. Who was he? I wondered, and what was all that about his replacement? What kind of madman was it out there who wanted to kill him?

In the stillness that followed the outburst, a scratch at the window made me turn around. A tiny, brown bird was sitting on the window sill and, as I watched, it flew up into the eaves and disappeared from view. Immediately, I thought of Winter's small bird tattoo on her wrist, and the 'Little Bird' inscription on the back of her locket. Frustration rose up my spine. I'd been so close to finally making some sense out of everything and now I was a prisoner in this place, with no prospect of escape. I was trapped. Hopeless. Useless.

7:20 am

I turned my attention to the notes on the chart at the bottom of my bed. According to these, I was extremely dangerous. I didn't know what 'Level 5 Restraints' were, but I didn't like the sound of them.

An overwhelming feeling of claustrophobia came over me and I ran to the door. Shivering in the hospital pyjamas, I grabbed the handle and twisted it with both hands—but of course it was locked and wouldn't budge. I shuffled away to the other side of the dingy, high-ceilinged room, near the window, and kicked the wall in frustration.

I stared back at the door. Anger surged through my body and I took a running jump at it, throwing my body against it. I hit it hard and fell back onto the floor like a rag doll. After a few seconds I crawled back up to my feet and started banging.

But no-one came. Just like that orderly had said: you can scream all you like—nobody cares. After I'd exhausted myself, I stopped. Strait-jacket, I remembered.

7:36 am

Tired and cold, I pulled the blanket off the bed and wrapped it around me. I needed to clear my head, and shake off the building anger. This sort of mindless fury was not helpful. I remembered Repro's warning about irrational people making fatal errors. I thought of him in his secret lair behind the filing cabinets—he'd made a secure little home for himself and I envied him.

I shuffled to the window once more and peered up through the glass beyond the bars. That's when I noticed a tiny mud nest attached to the eaves. I could just make out the shapes of baby birds with their beaks wide open as the mother bird arrived and perched on the edge of the nest.

Crazy as it sounds, I even resented those little birds. They had a home—they were safe.

I looked down into the dim garden, deserted now at this early hour, desolate and forbidding in the grey light. Standing by the window, I felt the full force of my loss. I'd even been deprived of stuff like my phone, my clothes, the guardian angel pin that Repro had given me. I didn't have the little Celtic ring anymore, but at least that was with Gab.

On top of all that, my identity had been stripped from me. The chart said I was supposed to be 'Ben Galloway'.

The muffled chirping of the little birds took my attention again. Diamond-shaped beaks greedily gaped wide, as each one tried to push the others away in an effort to get to their mother's food first.

The sight of the littlest one barging in from the back of the nest, shoving past his much bigger brothers suddenly changed my mood and I switched my way of thinking. He was the smallest, but his determination took him to the front.

Right now I didn't have a plan—I didn't have a clue how I was going to get out—but I owed it to my family not to crash into despair. I was going to fight. I sure wasn't going to make it easy for my enemies by giving up. From now on, I promised myself, I'd be always on the lookout for a gap in security.

I threw myself back on the bed. The lump on the back of my shoulder seemed to be getting bigger and was quite painful. But I had other things to worry about.

Think, Cal, *think*.

I desperately needed a plan.

8:23 am

I jumped at the sound of the door being opened. Someone in hospital greens shoved a tray through the door.

I went over to inspect breakfast—a blob of yellow and white that was supposed to be scrambled eggs, two leathery slices of toast and a cup of something like coffee. It all looked worse than army rations, but it was food, and I was starving. I grabbed the plastic spoon and tucked in.

9:03 am

The door to my room flew open and Musclehead, the big psych nurse—shaven head, a silver-lined hole in his earlobe—strode into my room.

'OK, son,' he said, 'put your clothes on. Dr Snudgeglasser will see you now.'

The nurse threw my clothes at me and waited while I pulled them on.

It felt really good to be wearing my own clothes again, and I was relieved they hadn't thrown them in an incinerator. Putting on my jeans, T-shirt, hoodie and sneakers—even without the shoe laces—made me feel more human, more myself.

So, I thought, I'm going to find out who Dr Snudgeglasser is. Maybe this doctor would be able to help me—if I could just convince him that I wasn't Ben Galloway.

9:07 am

Musclehead kept a firm grip on my arm while he led me downstairs and along a corridor of doors that were the same as the one on my room—heavy and bolted. All the time my eyes were scanning, looking for a chance to escape. At the end of the corridor were glass double doors, with people coming in and out. I knew if I got a chance I'd bust through those doors and be on my way to freedom.

9:10 am

We stopped in front of a door that stood out from

the others. It was wooden and unnumbered, and didn't have the thick you're-never-getting-out-of-here bolt locking it. Musclehead knocked and then pushed me through, closing the door once more behind me.

I looked around. I was in a cosy, sun-filled office with cream-coloured walls, tall with bulging bookshelves, and a big desk near a wide window. Framed qualifications hung in the spaces that were not covered by shelving. I noticed that there were papers on the desk weighed down by a small brass moulding of a brain.

On my side of the desk was a small, straight-backed chair, while behind it, and turned away from me on an elaborate leather armchair, was a broad-shouldered figure.

'Hello?' I said.

The figure swung round—a man in a tweed sports jacket, with bushy eyebrows, black-rimmed spectacles and a stern expression in his dark eyes.

So this was the doctor that one of the other patients had been threatening this morning. I stood in front of him, feeling as if I'd been called to the principal's office.

'I'm Dr Snudgeglasser,' he said. 'Please sit down.'

He gestured to the chair in front of me, before picking up the brain paperweight and leaning back in his armchair. I sat down and checked out the row of funny little spiky cactus plants on his desk.

There was a silence until Dr Snudgeglasser put down the brain he'd been toying with and looked over the tops of his glasses at me.

'You know why we're here.'

'Actually, I don't,' I said.

He picked the brain up once more and rolled it around in his hand.

'I've been kidnapped,' I said. 'Someone stuck a tranquillising dart in my neck and the next thing I know I'm here. Locked in a cell.'

Dr Snudgeglasser wrote something down before looking up again. 'The patients' quarters are certainly not cells,' he said. 'That's a very dramatic narrative, Benjamin.'

Benjamin. This stranger's name made me feel really uneasy, but I ignored it. 'Dramatic or not, it's what happened.'

'I see,' he said, in a way that sounded like he didn't see at all.

I watched him twist the brain in his fingers. I gripped the arms of the chair that I sat on, trying to stay cool. It didn't seem like there was any hope of escaping Dr Snudgeglasser's room. His window wasn't covered by bars, but it was sealed the whole way around. He had a button on his desk, too, which I'm sure meant he could call for help or assistance when faced with a particularly difficult patient.

Dr Snudgeglasser sighed.

'Ben,' he started.

'My name is not Ben.'

He ignored my interruption.

'Ben, I'm a psychiatrist. You have already been assessed. I have all your details, and I'm here to help you. We both need to be honest with each other. I can't do my job, and *help* you, unless you admit to me who you really are. Mr Sligo wants you to be helped, but I can't work with someone in denial.'

Sligo. I gritted my teeth, trying to hide my fury.

'I need to relate to the real *you*,' Snudge-glasser continued, 'otherwise I'm just joining you in your delusion. Do you understand?'

I didn't, but I thought it better not to say so.

'Maybe you should read Mr Sligo's letter. It was given to me when you were admitted here two days ago. It might help you come to terms with your position.'

The doctor tilted his head like he was trying to read me. He handed over the letter.

Dear Alistair

As previously discussed, I will be paying for Ben Galloway's expenses until such time as he is cured of his delusions and ready to hand over the documents he is wrongly withholding.

I have a great deal of respect for your work and interest in your hospital and hope this is evident in my financial support. I'm very confident that your expertise will help Ben come to accept the truth. As you know, his father and I were in business together for many years. Once young Ben has come to his senses, admits his true identity, and agrees to hand over certain documents that his father—may he rest in peace—entrusted to me, I will be delighted to donate further to Leechwood Lodge and, of course, continue to support Ben in whatever endeavour he chooses. Until then, I will continue to pay all expenses because of my unswerving loyalty to his father.

It was wonderful to see you at the premiere of 'Swan Lake' last week.

Yours sincerely,

Vulkan Sligo

Vulkan Sligo

I passed the letter back to him. My mind was going into overdrive. Why would Sligo go to all the trouble and expense of hijacking me and locking me up here to undergo expensive psychiatric treatment? Someone like Sligo doesn't do anything without a reason—a reason that brings big benefit to him. If he already had Dad's drawings, the text of the Ormond Riddle, the transparency with the two names and all my other papers, there'd be no reason to put this sort of pressure on me. Why not just get rid of me? It made no sense . . . It only made sense if . . .

If Sligo didn't have the drawings or the Riddle!

He was clearly behind my abduction, but he *didn't* have any of my stuff!

My feeling of elation was short lived. If he didn't, then who did? Maybe Oriana de la Force's thugs had swooped on the boathouse and taken my things. Sligo, not knowing that the other gang already had the goods, must have sent his gorillas after me and was holding me here at Leechwood until I handed the drawings and the Riddle over to him, or revealed where they were.

'What do you have to say about the matters raised in Mr Sligo's letter, Ben?' Dr Snudge-glasser's voice interrupted.

I wasn't sure what I should say. I hesitated. If I told the truth about not knowing where the documents were, he probably wouldn't believe me. And if he did believe me, I would become useless . . . and what would Sligo do with me then?

Dr Snudgeglasser held the metal brain in his fist and tapped it on the desk, impatiently.

'Sligo has made this whole thing up because he wants to get hold of something that my father gave *me*. Something that doesn't belong to him and is none of his business. He has *never* been in partnership with my father,' I snapped.

I was going to add that Sligo had already tried to kill me, but I decided to be quiet about this for the time being. Dr Snudgeglasser might just see that accusation as another 'dramatic narrative' and another display of my craziness.

'So it's true he wants something of your father's?'

'Yes, but it's not what you're thinking. It was given to *me. Me*,' I repeated, 'not Ben Galloway. He's made up this story about my delusions because he's trying to get his hands on something that doesn't belong to him.'

'You're accusing Vulkan Sligo of concocting a completely false identity and history for you?'

'That's right, Doctor, I am.'

'You're not Ben Galloway?'

'Damn right, I'm not!' I shouted. 'Sligo's made this whole thing up, and you've swallowed it, hook, line and sinker!'

Dr Snudgeglasser shook his head and shuffled his chair back a few centimetres. He gave me a kindly look as if I'd just proven that I was delusional, and then picked up a large envelope, the contents of which he tipped out onto his desk. He pushed the first document towards me.

'Reality check, Ben,' he said. 'I want you to have a good look at these. This is your birth certificate, your passport and here is the rest of your ID. Take them with you. All this, I suppose, is false too?'

I snatched the documents from him and flicked through them. They looked frighteningly genuine to me, and had my picture on many of them.

'That's not me,' I said handing the passport back to him, 'and that's not my birthday, either.'

'And this is your school travel ID,' he continued, as if I hadn't spoken at all, passing me a wallet. I flipped it open. I couldn't believe what I was seeing—an ID with my photo next to Benjamin Galloway's name.

STATE TRAVEL PASS

Benjamin Galloway
15 Oakland Drive,
Pearl Point 3054

STUD002052

STATELINK TRANSIT

'That's not me!' I shouted. 'I've never lived there in my life!'

There was something really freaky and terrifying in seeing myself remade as someone else. Already I felt so far away from my old life. I was forgetting what Mum's happy face looked like and what it had been like living at home with Gab and Dad before he died, and before I had to go on the run, fighting to stay alive. This Ben

Galloway wasn't me, but it was starting to feel like the old Callum Ormond wasn't me either.

The doctor started tapping the brain on the desk again. 'That's not you? In the picture?'

'No,' I said. 'I mean, yes. But . . .'

'Ben, let me refresh your memory. Your father, Redmond Galloway, was Mr Sligo's business partner. He died in tragic circumstances, I understand. It's not easy to accept something like that.' He waved the passport at me. 'Do you deny this is your photograph?'

I couldn't deny it; it was me in the photo. I even remembered exactly when it was taken, with Mum and Gabbi in one of those little booths at the local shopping centre about a year ago. It just wasn't my passport or my name.

'That's my photograph,' I said.

Had someone stolen my photos and passport during the break-in at our house in January? Had they then doctored them to create this false identity?

'That's my photograph,' I said again, 'but the rest is rubbish. They're not my IDs.'

'So you would have me believe that Mr Sligo has gone to all this trouble and created a completely false identity for you, using your photos, so that he can get hold of something that you have—something that he is *not* entitled to?'

'That's *exactly* what I'm saying. You've heard of identity theft? I remember when this photo was taken,' I said, pointing at the passport. 'And someone, somehow, has used it to create this totally insane and false identity, to get Sligo what he wants.'

'Why on earth would he do that? Have you any idea how difficult and expensive it is to create false passports?'

'Not if you have enough money and the right contacts. The right *criminal* contacts. And if you're the sort of person who will go to any lengths to get what you want.'

Dr Snudgeglasser sighed loudly. 'Ben, this is clearly paranoia. What you're claiming doesn't make sense.'

'It does make sense! After my dad died, we—'

'So you admit that your father has passed on?' Dr Snudgeglasser quickly interjected.

'Yes, he died, but *Redmond Galloway* is not my father. Because *I* am not Ben Galloway!'

I was in an impossible situation. Totally lose-lose! If I admitted who I was, Cal Ormond, the nation's most wanted criminal, I was in just as much trouble as I was by denying the false identity of Ben Galloway. Either way, I lost out. Either way I'd be locked up. In the asylum or the slammer.

'If you're not Ben Galloway, then who are you?' asked the doctor.

I squirmed uncomfortably in my seat, not knowing what to say. The thought of being arrested seemed like a better deal right now. I could try to make a break for it while I was being picked up by the police. I was thinking that I'd rather take my chances with the cops than stay locked up here in Leechwood at the mercy of Vulkan Sligo.

Sligo and Snudgeglasser had me squeezed in a vice.

'Well?' he demanded.

'I'm Callum Ormond,' I mumbled, finally.

The doctor leaned back in his chair and ran a finger over his bushy eyebrows. I started worrying that I'd made the wrong decision by confessing my true identity. I'd spent the last few months hiding who I was, and now I was offering it up freely.

I looked up to see that the doctor seemed completely uninterested and unmoved by what I'd said. He appeared more frustrated than anything else.

'Call the police,' I said, feeling desperate. 'They're all looking for me. They'll know who I am.'

'The police?' Dr Snudgeglasser asked, dubiously peering at me.

'Go on,' I urged. 'Call them! They'll tell you who I am!'

'I agree,' Dr Snudgeglasser continued, 'now that you mention it, that you bear *some* resemblance to that wanted lad. But taking refuge in this absurd story that you're some sort of fugitive wanted by the police rather than face the truth is not going to help you get out of here.'

'I look like him because I *am* him!' I shouted, thumping my fist on the desk. My shoulder twinged with pain and I automatically grabbed it with my left hand. It felt sore and swollen.

'I am him,' I said again, this time calmly.

Dr Snudgeglasser kept talking. 'You're just taking advantage of the similarity to create this complete confabulation.'

'Confabulation?' I guessed the meaning of this word. Dr Snudgeglasser believed I was making it all up. I tried another tack. 'You must know that Vulkan Sligo is a criminal. He is notorious. Everyone knows that! He'll lie to get whatever he wants!'

'He has never been convicted of any crime,' said Dr Snudgeglasser, adjusting his glasses. 'The media is largely responsible for the sensational reports about him—most of them quite without foundation. He has a number of court cases pending with various media outlets, defending his good name and reputation against their slanders and libels. He has been a great friend to Leechwood with his financial support.'

I recalled the terrifying night in the car yard when I was trapped inside the underground oil tank, and about to drown or suffocate. There was nothing sensational or made up about that.

I realised it was useless to try to convince him of the truth about Sligo. I understood the threat in the letter he'd written very well—I was going to have to stay in this place until I gave Sligo what he wanted. I also understood why I was supposed to be Ben Galloway—my real identity would create too much of a problem. Once the asylum knew who I was the police would pounce and I would be out of Sligo's reach. By giving me a false identity, he could keep me here safely and work on me until I handed over Dad's drawings and the Ormond Riddle. Except that I didn't have them any more! I had no illusions about what would happen when Sligo finally realised this; Ben Galloway *and* Cal Ormond would both simultaneously disappear for good.

'I need to call a friend urgently,' I said. 'I need to phone someone.' I was desperate to contact Boges. Maybe he could help me find out where all the documents were.

'All in good time, Ben,' said the doctor, insisting on calling me by my 'real' name. 'Our hospital works on a system of rewards. Good behaviour earns you privileges, like being allowed to make phone calls, outings in the garden, and, later, even visits to town. It's not a prison, Ben. You're here to get help. We're here to give you that help. So please, let's talk about you, Ben.'

'My name's not Ben,' I said again. 'Sligo is lying about everything. If you want to hear what I have to say, then let me tell you who I really am and what has happened to me.'

Dr Snudgeglasser's leather armchair squeaked as he leaned back again. He made himself comfortable as if he were waiting for a stage performance. 'I suppose we can do it this way for a while,' he said. 'I am rather interested to hear what you have to say.'

'OK. I guess it all began with a letter my dad sent me from Ireland.'

'Go on,' Dr Snudgeglasser nodded.

'Dad said that he'd come across something amazing in Ireland—some astounding secret that would change history and make our family rich.'

Dr Snudgeglasser nodded again.

'Then all these things happened. Bad things. My dad got really sick in Ireland. He came back home but died not long after from a mysterious illness—some unknown virus that made it impossible for him to even speak to us. In the hospice, he left behind all these strange drawings that he drew for me—my last clues into the discovery he'd made and mentioned in his letter. And then my uncle and I nearly drowned at sea, because someone had sabotaged our boat. Then there was a break-in at our house. Something was taken from Dad's luggage, and I found this transparency with two odd words written on it.'

Dr Snudgeglasser stopped nodding and started making notes. Maybe I was getting through to him. Or maybe I was digging myself deeper into trouble.

I felt I had no choice but to go on.

'I also found a mention of this medieval riddle—the Ormond Riddle—and, of course, there was the Angel.'

'An angel?' frowned Dr Snudgeglasser, stopping his scribbling for a moment. 'Are you saying you've seen an angel?'

'Yes,' I said, before seeing the look on his face. I couldn't help but roll my eyes. 'I'm not saying I saw an actual angel. It was a drawing, at first, but now I know there's this Angel associated with our family. There's an image of it in a stained glass window at the Memorial Park cenotaph, in honour of a distant relative, Piers Ormond, who died in the war. It's got something to do with what my dad discovered in Ireland.'

Even to me, what I was saying sounded pretty strange.

'Do go on,' invited Dr Snudgeglasser.

'After the break-in I was about to meet up with this woman who I thought could help me, when I was grabbed and thrown in a car boot.'

The doctor stared blankly at me as I spoke, as though I were about to reveal far-fetched tales of an alien abduction.

'I found out later that the kidnappers were led by Oriana de la Force.'

'The criminal lawyer?'

'Yes! Exactly! She had me tied up and she questioned me over and over. I managed to escape the closet they locked me in, and ran away. Then one day, not long after, I came home and someone had attacked my little sister and shot my uncle. I gave Gabbi CPR and then had to run again because there were people after me. I couldn't believe it when I heard the reports that I was the attacker! I had criminals after me, and the cops! I've been running for my life ever since!

'I was thrown in an oil tank to drown—

by your "great friend" Vulkan Sligo. I've been living under bridges, in sheds, in underground tunnels . . . I've been shot at, chased, bitten by a snake—'

'Attacked by a lion . . .' the doctor added, with a patronising grin.

I glared at him.

'I've read the stories, too,' he said by way of explanation.

'It all happened. To *me*.'

My voice petered out.

Dr Snudgeglasser put down his pen. 'That is certainly some story.'

'It's not a made-up story! It's what happened! I know I didn't tell it very well because it's so complicated and so much has happened, but it's all true! I've lived it!'

I could see he didn't believe a word of what I said.

Here I was, finally making a full confession of my real identity, and this doctor didn't believe me! Dr Snudgeglasser was convinced by the false passport and documents Sligo had tampered with.

'Interesting,' he continued. 'That was all very interesting. It teaches me even more than I know already about the human capacity for denial—to think that you would create such an amazing story rather than face the truth. Most intriguing. Perhaps Mr Sligo should invest in your writing career,' he chuckled to himself.

I sprang to my feet, furious. Dr Snudge-glasser's hand moved as fast as a snake strikes, to hover over the panic button on his desk.

I was beaten, I knew it. He was probably a decent man, underneath the arrogance and the eyebrows, but he was never going to believe me. Who would? I sank back in my chair.

'Vulkan Sligo is a crook,' I said, waving my hand over the false documents. 'Please believe me. None of this is true.'

Dr Snudgeglasser withdrew his surprisingly shaky hand from the panic button on his desk.

'Ben, attacking the person who is trying to help you is not going to help your case. You must face the truth—horrible though it is. This fantasy of yours is keeping you sick. Ben—'

'I'm not Ben!' I yelled, frustrated and angry.

'—this elaborate fantasy of yours,' he continued as if I hadn't spoken, 'all this talk of riddles and attempts on your life, assaults by lions and snakes, sabotaged boats, history-changing secrets, all this is indicative of the terrible confusion and denial in your mind— your desperate attempts to avoid facing reality. This denial is delaying the healing process.

You *must* face the fact that your father is dead.'

'I'm not denying that! But it's *my* father who's dead, not the father of this fictitious Ben Galloway!'

'Listen to what you're saying. In one breath you admit that your father is dead, and in the next you deny it again,' Dr Snudgeglasser leaned across his desk. 'There's no need for you to create this paranoid escape. It's classic avoidance and it will not help you. You're similar to one of our more disturbed patients, Vernon. Poor fellow thinks he wants to kill me. He thinks I'm no longer me. Thinks I've been "replaced" by some foreign being.'

I remembered the yelling earlier this morning coming from down the corridor.

'That's what's happened to *me*!' I shouted. '*I*'ve been replaced! By this false ID!' I banged down on the phoney documents with my fist.

'Calm down, Ben. Vernon can't face the truth either. It's not me he wants to kill. It's the *truth* he wants to kill. You both have similar problems.'

I'd only made things worse, trying to explain. I could have howled with frustration and anger. But all that would earn me was a straitjacket. I controlled my temper by taking a few deep breaths.

Dr Snudgeglasser had a lot of fancy theories, I thought. But he was the one who couldn't see the truth in front of him.

'You must grieve, Ben,' he said. 'You must grieve before you can heal. You need to welcome the healing process. Death is a part of life that we all must go through.'

'I don't need a healing process!' I said, leaping uncontrollably out of my chair again. 'I just need to get out of here!'

Dr Snudgeglasser's hand shot out and pressed the red button firmly. An orderly bounded through the door and before I could jump out of the way he grabbed me and hauled me into the corridor. I kicked and yelled and tried to break free from his grip as he dragged me like a sack of potatoes down the hospital hall.

'I'm not Ben Galloway!' I screamed, kicking and struggling. 'I'm not! I'm Cal Ormond! I'm the Psycho Kid! I'm the Psycho Kid!'

Another voice from behind a locked door joined me in my screaming. '*I'm* the Psycho Kid!' he shouted. 'I am!'

Another deep voice joined in. 'No! I am! I'm the Psycho Kid!'

'I'm the Psycho Kid' cried another guy in a straitjacket who, like me, was being dragged down the hallway, past me.

It was hopeless. All these voices clamouring and shrieking, copying my words, reduced me to silence.

As I was hauled away, back to my cell, the squabbling voices faded. I was starting to see that in this place, the truth was nothing but another delusion.

5 MAY

241 days to go . . .

8:02 pm

It didn't take me long to realise that I had to accept the false identity and play along with being Ben Galloway if I ever wanted to get out of Leechwood. I needed to get on the road, find all of my things again, and find my great-uncle Bartholomew for information on my dad's discovery. Owning the false identity could have its upside, too: it could give me an alias.

The few days I'd been at the asylum already felt like a month. Most of the time I stayed in my room, where the only distractions were the regular meals brought in on a tray by the biggest orderly, or staring through the bars at the damp gardens outside.

Occasionally Vernon would cause a stir, yelling out his death threats against Dr Snudge-glasser. I tried to keep my mind on the job—going over the progress we'd already made, but it was almost impossible to focus in this place when I had no idea whether I'd ever be able to get out.

Some of the weird events of the last month— my attempt to get to Mount Helicon to see my great-uncle, my terrifying night in the bush trying to evade Oriana de la Force's thugs and stray bullets, followed by meeting Melba Snipe and the runaway guy Griff Kirby—all seemed like a wild dream. For a moment I wondered if all of that had happened to someone else—to the guy who looked exactly like me. My double. Maybe *he* was Ben Galloway.

No. That didn't make sense either.

9 MAY

237 days to go . . .

3:31 pm

I was back in Dr Snudgeglasser's office, staring at the row of cactus plants again.

'How are you feeling this afternoon?' he asked.

'Pretty good,' I said, sighing. 'A little more like myself.'

Dr Snudgeglasser looked very pleased. 'That's good, Ben.'

He passed me the passport, the school bus pass and the birth certificate. 'Please don't reject these. Make sure you put them somewhere safe—there are some strange people in here.' He laughed at his little joke. 'Now the next thing to consider, now that you're becoming more reasonable, is the other documents you're holding. The papers that Mr Sligo requires. You've been here over a week now. Perhaps you are more inclined to hand them in?'

'I haven't got them any more,' I said. 'I did

have them with me, but my place was broken into and they were stolen. Right now, I don't know where they are. Sounds like a sketchy story, but it's the absolute rock-solid truth.'

Dr Snudgeglasser sighed and drew back, picking up a pen and fiddling with it. 'I can see this is going to be a long, drawn-out process, Ben.'

'Why don't you let me out of here,' I suggested, 'so that I can go after the documents? I have an idea where they might be. I can't hand them over if I don't know where they are.'

Dr Snudgeglasser picked up an envelope from his desk, took a letter out, unfolded it and then looked over the top of it at me. His glasses glinted in the afternoon light.

'It's not possible to let you out just yet. I was hoping I wouldn't have to tell you this, but I've realised there is no point in mystifying you. You seem to think that you've been locked up here for no real reason. Ben, that doesn't happen at Leechwood. This is the twenty-first century—and this is a best-practice, modern therapeutic centre, and not some Gothic prison in a horror story. Here's something else you need to read and accept.'

DR MANFRED OPPENHEIMER (M.B.B.S)

Dear Alistair,

Ben Galloway was referred to me because of his violent rages, which have already endangered people close to him, not to mention complete strangers.

I have been advised that prior to his father's death he had a calm and passive personality, without any history of violence or aggression. In my previous experience with Ben, he has always been a most pleasant fellow. It is my belief that his denial of the death of his father is at the root of his violent rage, and that as soon as he can acknowledge what has happened and release this grief, the rage will subside.

Dr Manfred Oppenheimer

'You see, Ben. It's not just Mr Vulkan Sligo who is concerned about you. You've been referred to me by one of the greatest physicians in the country. Dr Manfred Oppenheimer is the leader in this field, Ben. So why don't you do what he suggests? Do you really think that there is some sort of complex conspiracy to keep you here?'

'That's *exactly* what I am saying! I don't know about this Dr Manfred Oppenheimer—I've never heard of him! That letter could have been written about somebody else and Ben's name written in later. The whole thing could be a forgery, just like all the "Ben Galloway" IDs with my photo on them. Sligo could have paid the doctor to write it! Or threatened him to write it! He's the one who tried to kill me—he's the one who's violent!'

Dr Snudgeglasser took his glasses off, frowned, polished them and put them back on his nose. I realised instantly I'd made a mistake again by denying that I was Ben Galloway.

'Right,' he sighed patiently. 'I'm getting the feeling you've been very dishonest with me. I'm getting the impression that you're pretending to be Ben Galloway to please me. It often happens between therapists and their patients.'

I sprawled back hopelessly in the chair, floored by the impossibility of my situation. If

I said I was Cal Ormond, I was delusional. If I admitted to being Ben Galloway, Dr Snudgeglasser would think I was only saying that to please him.

I took a deep breath and began backtracking.

'I didn't mean to give that impression. It's just . . . it's very confusing coming out of all this denial and delusion. I know I *am* Ben Galloway,' I lied. 'And Redmond Galloway was my father.'

I decided to stretch the act a little further. I leaned my elbows on the desk and let my head fall into one of my hands.

'Everything that's happened has been so hard,' I sighed, letting my eyes glaze over. 'My dad dying,' I said quietly, looking down, 'was the toughest thing. Old Red. I miss him so much. He meant the world to me. He was like a best friend. Sometimes it all hurts so bad that I don't want to be me any more.'

I suddenly felt my eyes stinging with real tears, but I fought them back. Perhaps I wasn't putting on such an act after all.

Dr Snudgeglasser leaned forward and tapped the ID. 'Thank you for opening up, Benjamin,' he said quite sincerely. 'I do understand your confusion, and your loss. And I'm here to support you, not to cause you further suffering.'

He relaxed back in his chair, swivelling it a

little from side to side, frowning as he looked at me from under his bushy eyebrows.

'Ben,' he said quite gently, 'you must give your late father's papers to Mr Sligo.'

'I feel really bad about that,' I said, 'but I already told you, I don't have them. I honestly don't have them. They were stolen from me.'

'Stolen?'

'Yes, stolen.'

It was the one honest thing I was saying, and yet on hearing this, Dr Snudgeglasser already seemed to have lost the kindness from a moment ago and returned to his former suspicious self.

'Ben, this will not help you. You must realise your position. This resistance is not helping your case at all.'

'I'm telling the truth. They were stolen.'

Dr Snudgeglasser looked frustrated and disappointed, perhaps in himself for thinking that 'Ben Galloway' was finally coming around.

'OK,' he said, resolved to the fact that I was a liar.

My effort had achieved absolutely nothing. I stood up and pushed my chair away.

'You can't just keep me here as if I'm a prisoner. I want out of here! Why don't you call Dr Oppenheimer? He'll tell you he's never even met me!'

144

'I see,' Dr Snudgeglasser replied. 'You are suggesting that we're all involved in the conspiracy, eh? To harm you?' He shook his head. 'I've already checked with Dr Oppenheimer. I called him when you first arrived. It's part of my job to talk to the other physicians who have tried to help you. We're all trying to help you. And Manfred confirmed exactly what his letter says.'

It was hopeless. Sligo had every base covered.

'And don't think violence is going to get you anywhere,' he added. 'You know I have this emergency button right here that means the orderlies can be on you in seconds.'

'I'm not interested in hurting anyone,' I said. 'And there's nothing wrong with me. I just need to get out of here.'

'First, you concocted this fantastic story of being a runaway like that celebrity fugitive. You tried running away from the truth and seized that boy's story as a sort of cover—an emotional cover for your own story, which you still can't face. Ben, do you think that by holding on to the documents you're keeping your father alive in some way? That while you hold on to the documents, you hold on to your father too?'

It was strange how the doctor's words, which were meant for Ben Galloway, had so much meaning for *me*. I thought of all the hopes I'd pinned on the documents I'd been protecting. The pursuit of the truth about the DMO—the Dangerous Mystery of the Ormonds—had been keeping Dad alive in my mind. I didn't want to let that go. Ever.

'Your dad's gone,' he continued. 'He's dead. No documents are going to bring him back to you, and the sooner you realise that, the sooner you will get out of here.'

His words cut deeply. A fire rose inside me. I lurched at him over the desk.

Dr Snudgeglasser slammed the emergency button down, and kicked his chair away from me.

Within seconds, the door opened and the huge orderly with a shaven skull—Musclehead—came into the room and grabbed me.

'I think you're going to be with us for quite some time, Ben,' said the doctor, standing up and straightening his jacket. 'Please take Mr Galloway back to his room,' he said to the orderly.

'Any medication, Doctor?' asked Musclehead.

Dr Snudgeglasser looked at me. 'You'll behave yourself, won't you, Ben?'

4:14 pm

Musclehead put a heavy hand on my shoulder and steered me out of the room. He reminded me of a genie out of a bottle—all shoulders and upper body—huge—draped in hospital greens, with a prickly, shorn head and scowling face.

'Get a move on,' he said, giving me a shove in the corridor.

I'd really messed things up again, and didn't know whether I'd be able to recover Dr Snudge-glasser's trust. I had to try to get out. Halfway down the hall was the stairwell up to the first floor where my room was. From that point, I gauged the distance to the double doors to be about twenty-five metres. A plan was starting to take shape in my mind.

I walked along, all calm and docile, with Musclehead's hand heavy on my shoulder, until we were almost at the bottom of the staircase. But instead of taking the first step, I wrenched myself away from his hand with a spinning sideways jump, and took off, running as fast as I could along the slippery vinyl, heading for the double doors at the end of the corridor. I had taken the orderly completely by surprise.

'Stop that patient!' I heard him yell. 'Staff emergency! Dangerous patient on the loose!'

4:17 pm

I pounded along the corridor, barrelling past the curious staff members who had stepped out of their offices. A couple of them tried to grab me but I wrenched myself free. I ducked another orderly who suddenly appeared through the double doors and tried to seize me. But I pushed him away, throwing him off balance, and then I rocketed away past him.

I was almost at the double doors! Behind me I could hear the pounding of several staff members and by now a siren was blaring and red lights along the corridor ceiling were flashing.

I reached the doors and threw myself against them.

They opened! I was outside!

I leaped down the stairs and took off along the garden path that I'd noticed from my window. I knew this led to the main entrance, as I'd seen visitors entering and leaving the site through it. I hammered along the cement path, head down, legs pumping. The blaring sound of the alarm fuelled my adrenaline surge, adding speed and recklessness to my race. Out of the corner of my eye I saw one of the male nurses appear and try to crash-tackle me, but that just gave me an extra burst of speed. He grunted as he missed me and hit the deck, swearing.

I raced around a curve in the path, and ahead of me I saw the dark-green iron gates—solid iron with spikes along the top—but supported on either side by stone pillars.

Behind me, my pursuers were gaining ground. I threw myself at the gap between the gates and one of the pillars, my scrabbling fingers finding a handhold on the top hinges, while my bare feet clawed a foothold on the stone. I heaved myself forward and up, grasping the top of the pillar.

I had done it! I gave a shriek of triumph!

I barely noticed that I'd grazed my shins as I hauled myself up and over, dropping to the ground on the other side of Leechwood Lodge.

4:20 pm

I took off down the road. I didn't care where I was going—I didn't *know* where I was going! But I was out of there! I'd contact Boges, do whatever I had to do to get back the drawings and the Riddle, and then get the heck out of the city and on to my great-uncle at Mount Helicon.

I kept running and running, head down, arms pumping.

4:27 pm

The screeching brakes of the vehicle were the first I heard of its approach. The van pulled up beside me, jumped the footpath and slewed sideways, so that I nearly crashed into it. I almost screamed with frustration!

Musclehead and another orderly jumped out.

I tried running around the back of the van, but they pounced on me, pinning me on both sides, slamming me hard against the side of the vehicle.

Musclehead twisted my right arm painfully behind me.

'Nice try, sunshine,' he hissed into my ear. 'Move and I'll break your arm!'

14 MAY

232 days to go . . .

10:00 am

They kept me in the straitjacket for two long, painful days after my escape attempt. My plan had really backfired—I was now in a worse position—hemmed in by even more security.

The little birds outside had gone and the little mud nest had broken up and fallen away as if it had never even been there. Every morning, Vernon yelled his threats from down the hallway and I had nothing to do except try to ignore the noise and think about how I could get out. I had to change tactics.

Every day, my enemies might be getting closer to working out the meaning of the Ormond Riddle or interpreting Dad's drawings. A criminal lawyer like Oriana de la Force could have experts from anywhere in the world—code breakers and cryptographers. Right now they might be working on it, coming to grips with it, deciphering what the drawings and the Riddle meant. I felt an urgency that was close to panic—and I couldn't keep still.

I had to come up with a plan.

15 MAY
231 days to go . . .

8:02 am

When my breakfast tray arrived, I called out. It was a new nurse, a woman over six feet tall, who put her head around the door. The blue eyes and floaty blonde hair didn't fool me—I could see the steely hardness in her face. She looked tough, like the sumo wrestler's sister, only slimmer.

'Call me Gilda,' she said, in a most unwelcoming voice.

'I want to see the doctor,' I said. I needed to get out of this cell I was locked up in.

'All in good time,' Gilda said. 'You're allowed half an hour in the recreation room after lunch today. Dr Snudgeglasser hopes you'll stop this attention-seeking behaviour and do what is required, so don't mess up,' she warned. 'Things could always get much tougher for you.'

She left and locked the door again. I thought about the threat involved in her words. I had never been seeking the attention I'd attracted.

8:31 am

After I'd eaten breakfast, I stared out the window through the bars, pulling my hoodie up around my ears because of the chill in the air. I saw other patients in the garden and I could hear the sound of distant traffic. I had to get out—but not just into the recreation room, out of this asylum.

2:05 pm

Gilda collected me from my room. With an iron grip on my upper arm, she steered me downstairs.

'You see, Ben, it can be quite pleasant here—as long as you have certain privileges. TV, phone calls, even special treats like your favourite food. It's more like a hotel, for people who cooperate. Dr Snudgeglasser hopes you will cooperate. And so do I.'

This technique reminded me of Boges's earlier warning about good cop, bad cop. Was this an attempt to soften me up with alternating threats and bribes?

I walked with her into the recreation room. 'Take a seat,' she said before leaving, locking the door behind her.

The room was long and wide, with a few plastic tables and chairs, a TV, tattered board games and domino boxes, and some square floor cushions. A few patients were scattered around, busy with their own company, it seemed—none of them stirred as I passed by. I sat myself down by a table at the end of the room, under the windows. I noticed they were all locked, barred, and open only four or five centimetres at the top. They had what looked like silver security tape running around the edge of each pane of glass, holding wiring in place.

Cigarette burns dotted the table tops, and the scent of a eucalyptus-based disinfectant on the newly mopped floors hung in the air. I turned around as somebody else plopped down behind me.

'You're new,' he said, as I studied him. He was a pale, plump guy, with white eyelashes and strange eyes that seemed to look straight through me. He was a bit like a big baby, with a bald head and chubby cheeks.

Before I could say anything back to him, he scooted his chair closer to me, leaned in and whispered, 'They replaced my mother, you know.'

Was this Vernon, the guy Dr Snudgeglasser had talked about? The guy whose screams and threats thudded down the hallway on a daily basis? I frowned, puzzled, as he continued.

'She looked like my mother and she acted like my mother, but I knew the truth. It wasn't her. My real mother was imprisoned inside and I had to try and get her out.'

'And did you?' I asked, unsure of where this conversation was going.

He looked away, ignoring my question.

'Then they replaced my brother,' he began again. He nodded slowly. 'That's what they do. They replace people. Someone looks exactly like they used to, except they're not that person any more. You can see it in their eyes—they're not quite the same as they were before.'

I had no idea what to say, so I just listened to him.

'Dr Snudgeglasser. He's one of them—one of the replaced ones. I'm going to have to deal with it. His eyes are definitely different now.'

Something in his words made me very uneasy. This guy seemed quite clearly crazy, but I couldn't help thinking about what he was saying. It was too close to what had happened with my real identity being replaced with that of Ben Galloway.

Reality seemed to waver around me for a second as if it were nothing but a painted backdrop for a play. I looked around the place I was in. Was I going crazy? Was I in the right place? Had I been 'replaced' too?

Behind us, one of the patients suddenly turned up the TV to full volume. We both twisted around to see what was going on. He stood nearby clapping, while a few of the others in the room covered their ears, moaning.

I caught a glimpse of some football match highlights, before a glamorous newsreader's face filled the screen. I watched in disbelief as Uncle Rafe's house, with an ambulance in front of it, appeared on the screen. My jaw dropped. The newsreader's voice blared through the room.

'Police and paramedics were called to a Dolphin Point home earlier today where Mrs Winifred Ormond, the mother of the teenage fugitive, Cal Ormond, appears to have been the victim of a savage assault. Mrs Ormond was rushed to hospital after an incident involving an attempted burglary at the house she is currently residing in, believed to be shared with a relative. At this stage, police are unsure as to whether this incident is related to her son or not, but they cannot rule it out.'

I jumped to my feet, pointing to the screen.

'That's my mother!' I yelled over the volume of the TV, as I watched her being stretchered into the back of the ambulance. 'She's been hurt! I've gotta get to her!'

'Turn it down!' shouted a voice.

'Please, turn the TV down!' begged another.

'The juvenile, an attempted murder suspect,' continued the newsreader, 'has been on the run since January. Police have called for witnesses, and information from local residents, but warn members of the public not to approach Ormond if he is seen in the area, as he is believed to be armed.'

'Your mother?' shrieked the pale guy I'd been talking to before the TV was turned up. 'Are they replacing her too? We've gotta stop this! They're taking over the world!'

I could barely hear his words over the volume of the TV and the many shouts and moans to shut it off, but I watched as he ran to the door of the recreation room and began pounding on it, yelling at the top of his voice, 'They're taking over the world! Can't you see? Someone's got to stop them doing this, before we're all changed! Before it's too late!'

2:15 pm

Mum! Was she going to be OK? What had happened? Was Sligo guilty of this attack? Dr Snudgeglasser might have told him that I didn't have the documents, so Sligo could be turning his attention back on my family!

I started running towards the doors which had finally opened after the strange guy's hysterical thumping.

My blood was hot with rage and my head pounded so powerfully that it took me a few seconds to realise that the screaming of the patients, the blare of the TV and the thumping on the door had actually been taken over by an alarm siren ringing throughout the asylum.

The strange guy who'd been with me had bashed his way past whoever had opened the door and was now on the loose in a fit of rage. Somewhere, I could hear him yelling and throwing things around.

The place erupted in panic. Frantic footsteps ran in every direction. People were yelling out, their voices fused with the siren's wailing into a cacophony.

The door to the recreation room was swinging wide open, overlooked in the emergency! This could be my chance, I thought. I had to find my way to Mum!

Musclehead's hoarse voice yelled from down the hallway. 'Vernon's on the loose! Vernon's on the loose! Emergency stations!'

'And one of my carving knives is missing

from the kitchen!' screeched another voice.

I ran into the corridor where orderlies and nurses were flying in every direction. Gilda raced after Musclehead, and they all raced around after the big baby-faced guy who held the gleaming kitchen knife out in front of him. I seemed to have been forgotten. Perfect!

2:23 pm

Unnoticed, I ran to the glass double doors, but they were locked! Of course they would be— the place had gone into complete lockdown with Vernon on the rampage.

I wondered where Dr Snudgeglasser was, and as much as I disliked the guy, I hoped he'd locked himself away somewhere safe. Would Vernon try and free the 'real' Dr Snudgeglasser by using the knife? I shuddered at the thought.

The alarm was still screaming and I ran around in a frenzy as I tried to work out what to do. The reception office, halfway down the hall, had emptied for the chase.

I skidded into the office. This was my chance to contact Boges! I grabbed the phone. The line was dead! I couldn't believe it!

The desktop computer was humming away. I crouched over one of the keyboards, the ear-piercing siren filling my head and making it almost impossible to concentrate. My fingers were trembling with anxiety, but after fumbling a little I opened the email system.

I could hear voices again. The chase must be heading back this way! I had to be quick!

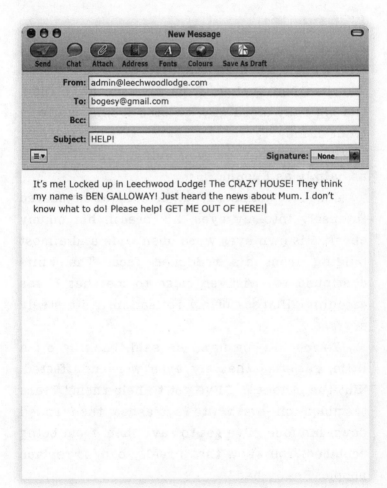

New Message

Send Chat Attach Address Fonts Colours Save As Draft

From: admin@leechwoodlodge.com

To: bogesy@gmail.com

Bcc:

Subject: HELP!

Signature: None

It's me! Locked up in Leechwood Lodge! The CRAZY HOUSE! They think my name is BEN GALLOWAY! Just heard the news about Mum. I don't know what to do! Please help! GET ME OUT OF HERE!

I was about to add more when I heard footsteps in the hallway coming even closer. I hit 'Send', deleted the email from the 'Sent' folder, and was halfway out of the seat when someone appeared at the doorway.

2:26 pm

I froze with fear when I turned and was met with a knife-wielding hand. The razor-sharp edge was just centimetres from my face as Vernon, the big baby-faced guy, twisted it unsteadily in front of me.

'Vernon, what are you doing, buddy?' I said as calmly as I could.

'Just . . . just checking,' he said, as he peered intensely into my eyes, his breath hot on my cheek. His own eyes were open wide and almost bulging from his reddened face. The knife continued to twist, so close to me that I was catching glimpses of my reflection in its steely surface.

'You're OK, for now,' he said, backing off a little, satisfied that my eyes were unaffected. 'But the others . . . I've got to help them.' Tears trembled on his white eyelashes then rolled down his face. 'I've got to save them from being replaced. You know that's really bad—to replace people. Really bad.'

'It is bad,' I agreed. 'I do know something about that, but maybe there's something else we could do about it together. What do you say?'

As well as feeling scared stiff, I was really sad to see him like this.

'Where is he?' asked Vernon, glancing round the office. 'Where's Dr Snudgeglasser?'

'He's not here,' I said. 'Maybe,' I said, trying to keep my voice from wobbling, 'it would be a good idea to put that knife down. If you want to warn people about being replaced, it's probably best not to scare them with knives.'

He looked down at the knife in his hand and then back at me.

There was a long moment when Vernon and I just stared at each other. He sniffed a bit and wiped his nose with the back of his other hand. But he still held onto the knife. There was no way I could get past him. Neither of us knew what to do next.

I realised then that Musclehead and Gilda had located us and were watching from the doorway, carefully working out a safe way to approach.

Vernon swung round at a small sound behind him, but it was too late. Musclehead and Gilda loomed up behind him and took him down. Another guy ran in, knelt on his back and wrenched the knife from his hand. I watched as the three of them dragged him towards the staircase. Vernon looked up at me with tearful eyes.

The way he looked at me with such sadness and desperation reminded me of the crazy guy on the street in Richmond who had first warned me about the Ormond Singularity, and surviving three hundred and sixty-five days . . . He'd looked at me with the same kind of fear and anguish in his face as he'd been dragged away by the paramedics.

2:36 pm

I'd just scraped through another day, alive. I staggered with relief and almost fell over a wheelchair behind me.

'What are you doing in here, Ben?' Gilda said, returning suddenly, alerted by the clattering of the chair.

'I didn't know where to run,' I said. 'I was scared. I was hiding from him.'

She hurried over to the phone and picked it up. 'He cut the phone line. Can you believe it?'

I held my breath. Would she still be able to find my email on the computer? I didn't think so. She gave me a long look, ordered me outside and locked the office door behind us both.

8:26 pm

It took a long time for everything to settle down after Vernon's wild siege, but eventually everyone was controlled and locked up back in their rooms. Including me.

Dinner came around quite late, but I didn't have much of an appetite. An eerie silence hung in the stale air. Who knew what they'd done with poor, delusional Vernon?

My brain felt like mush. Boges would be desperate to know where I was and I hoped he would find a way to help me before too long. I also hoped he was over our fight at the boathouse. I recalled his furious face, the two lines on his brow pulled into one angry furrow: 'I don't care how *cute* she is,' he'd yelled about Winter. 'Her friends have tried to kill you! What is it about attempted murder you don't understand?'

Then I recalled the scary scene I'd seen on the television newsflash—Mum lying on a stretcher with her eyes closed. Who would be checking in on Gabbi if Mum was in a hospital bed herself? Rafe? Where was he? Was he OK? My stomach was churning with anxiety and worry.

19 MAY

227 days to go . . .

2:53 pm

I was woken out of a restless sleep, where I'd been haunted yet again by the heartbroken wails of a baby and the dark sense of desolation at the core of my recurring nightmare. Someone was banging on my door. I struggled to find the energy to sit up in my bed—I'd wandered around like a zombie for the last few days, lost and without any sense of purpose.

I blinked as Gilda put her head around the door.

'It's nearly three in the afternoon! Time you got up, young man. You have visitors,' she said.

I sat up, suddenly nervous.

'Visitors?'

'Yes, visitors!' she said gruffly.

The picture of Mum being stretchered into the ambulance rushed back. What if Rafe had finally located me and had bad news for me about Mum?

'Are you surprised that your friends have come to visit you? Dr Snudgeglasser thinks it's a good idea—socialising, seeing your friends. Hopefully you'll remember the life you've left behind, Ben.'

'Friends?' I was puzzled. Gilda had used a plural. So it wasn't Rafe. But my relief was short lived. What if it was the sumo wrestler and Kelvin? Or Sligo? Or Oriana?

'What are their names?' I asked.

'I don't know!' she said. 'They're waiting for you in the recreation room. Hurry up and get dressed. But first, Dr Snudgeglasser wants to see you.'

2:59 pm

All the way down to the doctor's office, I worried about who these so-called friends were. Was I about to be attacked or dragged off to some other prison? I began preparing myself for anything.

At first Dr Snudgeglasser looked fatter than usual, but then I realised he was wearing a thick, panelled kind of protective vest under his sports coat. Vernon's recent rampage must have freaked him out.

'Ben,' he said, 'Vulkan Sligo obviously isn't the monster you believe him to be. He must

have confidentially contacted your friends
and informed them of your admission. Visiting
rights are a privilege here. And whether or not
you can see your friends will depend on your
cooperation.'

I wanted to tell him about seeing Mum on the
TV and why I had to get out, but stopped myself.
Right now I had to be Ben Galloway, obedient
and ready to do anything that Dr Snudgeglasser
or Vulkan Sligo might ask.

'I'll cooperate,' I said, sitting down in front of
him. 'Anything you say.'

'You have been very cooperative the last few
days, which means you're making good progress.
Are you willing yet to tell me the location of the
documents that Mr Sligo needs?'

I took a few moments to think carefully. If I
told the truth again, that I didn't know where
they were, I guessed I wouldn't be allowed to
see whoever these friends were. But to do that, I
had to come up with an answer that would please
Dr Snudgeglasser. I had a sudden inspiration.

'It's true that I don't actually have them right
now,' I said, 'but I do know who *does* have them—
Ms Oriana de la Force, solicitor. She's looking
after them.' I watched Dr Snudgeglasser writing
it down. 'Tell Mr Sligo. He could organise to pick
them up from Ms de la Force's office.'

Dr Snudgeglasser looked up at me.

'Not long ago you claimed Ms de la Force abducted you,' he said.

'I know. I lied, I'm sorry. I can't help myself sometimes. I get carried away, making up stories. But I'm not lying now. She has the documents. I have no reason to make that up.'

'I really hope that's right,' he said. 'For both our sakes, Ben.'

I wasn't sure if it was a good move or not, but it would put Sligo and Oriana de la Force at each other's throats, I hoped, and it would give me a little space.

Dr Snudgeglasser pressed the button on his desk and Gilda arrived to escort me away.

'You may see your friends, Ben,' said the doctor. 'But if this turns out to be another part of your confabulation, they'll be the last friends you see.'

I didn't like the sound of that.

3:17 pm

'Your visitors are waiting in the recreation room, Ben,' said Gilda as we walked down the corridor, her strong hand gripping my upper arm. 'I've got some reports to catch up on, but I'll be keeping an eye on you.'

The second I walked into the recreation room,

I saw the reason for the word 'friends'. A massive smile stretched across my face, and I realised I hadn't smiled in a long time.

3:20 pm

'Man, it is so good to see you!' I called out as I ran over to Boges, who was sitting at the table near the window. He jumped up and swung an arm around me.

'Dude, it is so good to see *you*!'

I stepped back and looked over to the other side of the table.

'Winter,' I said, confused about why Boges had brought her with him.

'Hi, *Ben*,' she said, using my fake name.

I remembered the last time I'd seen her at the cenotaph, right before Sligo's black Subaru turned up. Right before the boathouse was trashed and I was knocked out.

'She's cool,' said Boges, as if that should explain everything.

Winter was wearing big, red, heart-shaped sunglasses that hid the upper part of her face, but she slowly took them off, all the time holding my gaze. She had on a skirt and white Converse sneakers, and a knitted beanie over her long hair which flowed over the shoulders of a long, grey cardigan.

'So you got my email,' I said to Boges. 'One day I'll tell you what was going on when I sent it! I've been going crazy in here!'

'Cal,' he said quietly. 'We've been going crazy worrying about you. I even checked the car yard. I thought you might have been floating in an oil tank. Or floating face-down in the harbour. It is so good to see your ugly face.'

'Yours too,' I said. 'I'm alive, but I have to get out of here. What's happened to Mum?'

Boges and Winter looked at each other, carefully.

'Your mum is OK,' said Boges. 'I talked to Marjorie, your old neighbour, last night after she'd visited your mum. The police say she walked in on an intruder. She was knocked out— she needed a few stitches, that's all. She's still in hospital, but apparently she's coming home tomorrow. Then we'll get the full story. Don't worry about her. She's going to be perfectly fine.'

'But what about Gabbi?' I asked. 'And Rafe? Where was he?'

'Gab's OK. She still hasn't woken up, but she's getting there, I think. Rafe was out working when it happened. Lucky he wasn't there because he could have made it a lot worse if he'd tried to fight back.'

I nodded. 'Do they think I'm responsible for it?'

Boges looked awkwardly at Winter again, which was not a good sign.

'We don't know,' said Winter. 'The important thing for us is knowing who *was* responsible for it. Was it Sligo, or Oriana, or was it pure coincidence?'

Boges nodded in agreement with what Winter was saying. It was weird to see them getting along.

'I lost everything from the boathouse,' I said. 'We're going to have to—'

'Dude, chill,' Boges interrupted me, smiling. 'Everything's safe. It's all here!'

He leaned down and patted a backpack sitting on the floor near his chair.

'What are you saying?' I asked.

'I doubled back,' said Boges. 'After I left the boathouse I saw Sligo's car up on the street and knew trouble was coming. I watched you jump into the water and swim away, *without* your backpack. They got out of the car and headed off in your direction, so I snuck back to boathouse, grabbed everything I could from your bag and shoved it into mine. I was just swinging it over my shoulder when I heard them coming back. I didn't hang around, I can tell you. I was out of there faster than the speed of light!'

Winter smirked at him.

'You're a superhero now, are you?' she mocked.

'Hey! Enough of the insults, girl,' said Boges. 'And just when I'm starting to think that maybe you're not totally evil . . .'

She laughed and gave him a shove. I should have been happy they were getting along, but something annoyed me about the way they were suddenly so friendly. I tried to ignore it.

'Dude, you *are* a superhero,' I said, 'an absolute legend.' Such a massive weight had been lifted from my shoulders. I couldn't believe my mate Boges had been brave enough to go back and get my stuff for me.

'So tell us what happened to you,' Winter said taking off her beanie and cardigan. 'What's with the whole *Ben Galloway* thing?'

I gave them the quick rundown on how I'd ended up in Leechwood, how they were convinced I was Galloway—suffering from denial, and refusing to hand over documents to Sligo. I wrapped it all up with the story about Vernon and how I'd finally been able to send the SOS email.

'Seriously,' said Boges, 'I thought you were a goner. I hadn't heard from you in so long and had no idea what had happened to you. I thought

I saw Oriana's car near the boathouse, too. I didn't know what was going on, or who had taken you. For all I knew you could have fallen off a cliff!'

'Oriana? But it was Sligo who kidnapped me and chucked me into this place—despite some story about sending his thugs on a wild goose chase!' I glared at Winter.

'Hey, steady on,' said Boges. 'Listen before you shoot your mouth off too much. Winter's got a plan. To get you out of here.'

'Winter's got a plan?' I repeated.

'You could speak to me,' said Winter. 'I'm right here, you know.'

'As if I could forget,' I said, turning to her. 'I'm right here, too. Thanks to Sligo.'

Her dark, almond eyes looked straight into mine.

'Cal,' she said, 'I'm really sorry you're stuck in here. I don't know how Sligo got his hands on you. You have to believe I got into the car with Bruno and immediately led him away from you. I directed him back to the old squat. But there were new squatters there. I said they must have chased you away.'

I remembered again watching Winter sprint over to the car that was cruising near the gates of Memorial Park.

'So they think you're helping them out?'

'Yes, but I'm not. I'm helping you. And now we've gotta quit the chit chat and get you outta here.'

'Right,' nodded Boges.

With Winter and my best buddy with me, the world seemed a little less bleak.

'OK, so let's hear it,' I said.

Winter glanced over at Gilda, who was sitting at a table on the other side of the room near the door. Her head was bowed over the charts she was writing on and she seemed completely absorbed in her work.

'We've brought extra clothes. I have another set in my bag,' she said in a low voice, 'almost identical to what I'm wearing—'

'Minus the bells on the skirt,' Boges noted.

'And we have a wig for you,' she continued, 'the same colour as my hair.'

Cautiously, she opened the top of the embroidered bag. I leaned forward to see a mass of wild, dark hair sitting on the top of some clothes.

I looked at both of them. I felt my jaw dropping.

'You want me to dress like a *girl*?'

'You've got it in one,' Boges laughed.

'After you've gone to the bathroom to change, you'll just casually walk out with Boges,' Winter said. 'If you keep your head down and my sunglasses on, there's a very good chance no-one will take the slightest notice of you.'

Surreptitiously, she passed me her long cardigan, beanie and sunglasses. I noticed that she was wearing a hoodie, similar to the one I had on.

'But what about you?' I asked. 'What will you do once we're gone?'

'I thought you'd never ask,' she said, with a wry smile. 'You needn't worry about me. I'll stay nice and quiet right here, looking like I'm reading a book or something and by the time they work out what's happened, you'll be safely away.'

'And then?' I asked, imagining myself on the run in a skirt and wig.

'And then,' she repeated, 'I don't know. I'm pretty good at talking my way out of tricky situations.'

I ran the idea around in my mind. It was crazy, just crazy enough to work. I'd never have another chance like this one. I was jumpy with excitement and fear. But then I thought of something and turned to Winter.

'What about Sligo? He'll be furious when he hears about this. Especially your part in it.'

She gave me another one of her cool smiles.

'Leave Sligo to me,' she said. 'I'm not about to go and get myself in trouble. I know how to look after myself. I'm not stupid.'

'Come on, dude,' Boges urged, 'what are you waiting for?'

3:56 pm

At the back of the room were male and female toilets for the use of visitors. I discreetly pointed them out to Boges.

Slowly, Winter lifted the bag from her shoulders and quietly passed it to me, out of sight. I tucked it under my arm, stood up casually, then strolled to the back of the room towards the women's toilet, hoping there was no-one in there. Gilda looked up and then returned to her notes, without even noticing me.

In the toilet cubicle, I kicked off my jeans, T-shirt and hoodie, and awkwardly stepped into the purple skirt, pulling it up around my waist. I squeezed myself into the little black singlet and cardigan, and lastly pulled the wig on, tugging the two small tags on each side. It fitted tightly onto my head and I felt completely weird having long strands of wild hair hanging down my face. I hadn't worn a dress since I'd been a shepherd in a kindergarten play.

I grabbed the Ben Galloway IDs from my

jeans pocket and shoved them down the front of my top.

I stepped out of the cubicle, saw myself in the mirror and almost laughed! Once I'd put the heart-shaped, red sunglasses on, and pulled the knitted beanie down low over my forehead, it *could* have been Winter Frey staring back at me—*if* you didn't look too closely!

I hurried to the door of the toilets and opened it slightly, looking over to where Gilda was sitting, and where Boges and Winter waited, close together near the window, faces turned away. Winter had tied her thick, dark hair to the side, furthest away from sight, in a tight bun.

I walked over to the two by the window slowly, keeping my steps small.

Boges grinned, his eyes filled with amusement, as I sat beside him.

'Not bad at all,' whispered Winter, as she checked me out, too.

Gilda glanced over at us for a moment and then returned to her work.

'See? She hasn't noticed anything unusual,' Winter continued. 'Let's not waste any more time. I'll stay here while you two casually leave. Cal, don't walk so heavily. And don't take such big strides. By the way, you look great!'

'Like your double?' I joked.

Her expression immediately changed. 'No,' she whispered, shrinking back. 'Don't say that.'

I didn't have time to wonder why that idea freaked her out so much—my whole body was shaking with excitement at the possibility that we might just pull this off.

Boges stood up and made out like he was saying goodbye to me, except the 'me' was Winter, who stayed seated with her back to us.

'OK, *honey*, time you and I made tracks,' said Boges. He raised his voice a little for Gilda's benefit.

'See ya, Ben,' he waved. 'We'll be back again soon.'

We walked away and I waved back too in what I hoped was a girlie way.

Now for the last really tricky part, I thought, as we walked over to Gilda near the door. Boges had intentionally placed himself closest to her. She looked up as we approached and even smiled, nodding goodbye to us. Boges turned towards her and waved his arm, half hiding me from her view. I kept my head down as we stepped into the hallway.

4:20 pm

It took all my self-control not to break into a run as we neared the double glass doors. The orderly in the office near the exit looked up as we pushed through them. Boges kept casually chatting away to me. I had no idea, and didn't care, what he was saying—I was focused entirely on taking each step softly and convincingly. My heart was thumping and I could feel the sweat breaking out on my face.

4:23 pm

We stepped outside into the day and walked along together towards the tall green gates. Every moment, I was expecting to hear someone yell after me. I realised I'd been holding my breath almost since we'd said goodbye to Winter in the recreation room. I took a deep breath and Boges slipped an arm around my waist, slowing me down, because I was starting to hurry.

'Easy does it, sweetheart,' he said.

'Let's get out of here!' I hissed under my breath.

'All in good time, dude—or should I say dudette,' said Boges. 'We've made it this far, let's not mess it up now.'

4:26 pm

I was just starting to relax when I heard voices.

'Just act normal!' Boges commanded between gritted teeth.

'Let go of me! I gotta run! They're coming after me!'

'Hey!' called out a voice from behind us.

'I'm busted, Boges!'

I tore myself away from him and took off into the street, the purple skirt flying everywhere, the hair slapping me across the face as I ran, the long cardigan flapping in the wind.

But no-one tried to stop me, no-one came after me to tackle me down. The only person coming after me was Boges.

'It's OK!' said Boges, puffing up to me. 'She was just bringing this!'

I stopped and turned around to see an orderly in the distance, already on her way back through the entrance again. In Boges's hand was Winter's embroidered bag. I must have left it in the women's toilet. Luckily she hadn't asked Boges any questions about my odd dash down the street.

4:48 pm

As soon as we reached a group of shops I hurried into the public toilets and ditched Winter's clothes. I changed back into what I was wearing earlier, and threw on a new hoodie Boges gave to me.

'I think I liked you better the other way!'

joked Boges as I rejoined him outside.

'Too bad,' I said. 'Seriously, though, I can't believe I'm out. I thought I was going to be stuck in there forever. Thanks . . . for everything. You are the best buddy a guy could ever have.'

It was true. Boges was my anchorman. He was my only connection to my old world. He was my news channel, bringing me information about Mum and Gabbi. He was my lifeline. There were so many things that I owed him.

'Yeah, yeah,' said Boges. 'I just hope Winter made it out OK. Anyway,' he said, pulling his backpack off his shoulder, 'this is yours. All your dad's stuff is in there, plus the Riddle. There's some money in the back pocket, plus a new—well, a new *old*—phone. Your phone wasn't in your bag when I went back to the boathouse.'

'No, I had it on me. Leechwood Lodge has it now. You are the best,' I said, slinging the backpack on, wincing as it knocked against the tender spot on my shoulder.

'I know, I know. Just do me a favour and don't leave the bag behind again—ever. If Sligo gets hold of what you've found out already . . .'

'I'm disposable again, right?'

'I didn't want to say that,' said Boges.

'I know it. I haven't forgotten how quick he was to have me tossed in the oil tank. He's going to go psycho when he realises I escaped from Leechwood. And Winter could be dead for helping me,' I said, 'unless she's up to something herself. How will she explain it to him?'

'I don't think you need to worry about her,' said Boges. 'I don't think Sligo's going to find out. She knows how to look after herself. She is one smart babe. I'm almost starting to believe that she just *might* be playing for the right team.'

'But you still don't completely trust her?' I asked.

'I want to, and I'm pretty sure she's cool, but I don't fully trust people whose motives I don't understand,' Boges replied. 'Sligo's been her guardian—taken her under his wing after she was orphaned, given her a home—so why would she be so against him? Yeah, she knows he's a bad guy, but you'd think she'd be a little more . . . forgiving or something.'

5:23 pm

Before heading out to the highway, we ducked into a new internet cafe—Boges convinced me we'd be OK—and I checked my blog. There were heaps of new messages of support—I could hardly believe how many.

There were some shocking ones in there too. I stopped myself from reading most of them, but one guy's messages—a guy who called himself 'lock_him_up'—were pretty hard to ignore.

Web | Images | Video | News | Maps | More ⌄

Web Search

Hello, Callum

Contact Cal
Messages for Cal

| Write on Callum's Wall | Messages for Cal |

lock_him_up:

You are one sick human being. To think you've got yourself up here on this blog like you're some kind of celebrity! You should be ashamed of yourself, and so should all your 'fans'.

Callum Ormond is a killer! How can you support him? What if it was your little sister he put in a coma? And what if it was your uncle he'd shot? Would you all want to support him then? He's trodden all over innocent people to keep away from the law—people who have only tried to help him, like that Drysdale fellow who almost died in the Blackwattle Creek crash. He'd only offered him a lift out of the kindness of his heart.

Cal, you belong behind bars.

Web | Images | Video | News | Maps | More ▼

Web Search

Hello, Callum

Contact Cal
Messages for Cal

| Write on Callum's Wall | Messages for Cal |

J@s &T@sh:

hi cal

what's happened to you? you haven't posted any
messages for a while... we really hope you're ok
and hanging in there. please ignore lock_him_up,
and the rest of the nasty messages. we're on
your side because we think what you're saying
is true. we still believe in you. you're innocent.

xx

Web | Images | Video | News | Maps | More ▼

Web Search

Hello, Callum

Contact Cal
Messages for Cal

| Write on Callum's Wall | Messages for Cal |

 lock_him_up:

This kid deserves to be locked up,
and so do you for giving him this
ridiculous attention.

I felt gutted.

'Ignore it,' said Boges on seeing my reaction. 'You already know there are a lot of people who aren't behind you, but you have to focus on those who are on your side, and, more importantly, sorting this mess out so that you can prove your innocence. Quick, type up your message, and let's get off this blog.'

Web | Images | Video | News | Maps | More ▾

[   ] **Web Search**

Hello, Callum

Thanks for the supportive messages, guys. I can't answer you personally—but you know why. I'm OK, and I'll try and keep you up-to-date on what's going on when I can. Please keep believing in me, no matter what you might hear. And anything—anything at all—you think might help clear my name, please post it here, or send me a private message.

Contact Cal
Messages for Cal

Male
15 years old
Richmond

Inbox
Update Profile
Sign Out

POSTED BY TEENFUGITIVE AT 5:40 PM   0 Messages

'You finished?'

I nodded.

Boges pushed me out of the way, taking over

the computer. 'OK, I've got something to show you,' he said. 'I've drawn a bit of a blank on the last two lines of the Riddle, but I *did* find something that mentioned the Ormond Singularity.'

I leaned forward, watching while Boges hit a website.

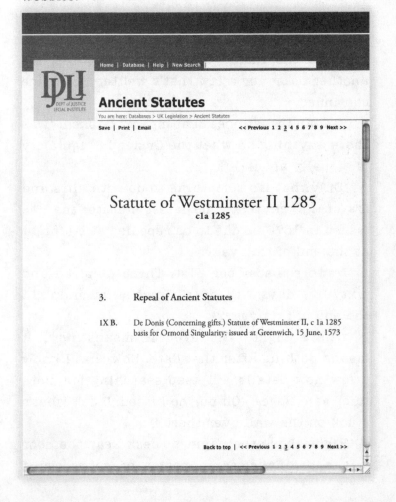

Home | Database | Help | New Search

Ancient Statutes

You are here: Databases > UK Legislation > Ancient Statutes

Save | Print | Email   << Previous 1 2 **3** 4 5 6 7 8 9 Next >>

Statute of Westminster II 1285
c1a 1285

3.   **Repeal of Ancient Statutes**

IX B.   De Donis (Concerning gifts.) Statute of Westminster II, c 1a 1285
        basis for Ormond Singularity: issued at Greenwich, 15 June, 1573

Back to top | << Previous 1 2 **3** 4 5 6 7 8 9 Next >>

'It was mentioned within all this stuff. Ancient statutes.'

'Statutes? Like laws?' I asked, as Boges scrolled down the Justice Department's website.

'Oh, someone's been listening in Legal Studies!' Boges joked as he clicked on a hyperlink. He stopped laughing, awkwardly, as we both thought about how long it had been since I'd seen the inside of a classroom. 'Yes, it's another name for a law that's written down,' he continued.

'OK, and what does that mean?' I asked. 'Was there anything on what the Ormond Singularity is actually about?'

'Only that it's something to do with gifts and it's on its way out. The latest statute, the one issued in 1573, is due to be repealed at midnight at the end of this year!'

I swore. December 31st. Three hundred and sixty-five days. 'It's over, finished, at midnight the end of this year?'

'That's right. Whatever it means now, it means nothing after that date. Now that I know a few new details, I'll keep searching for more info,' said Boges. 'Oh no,' he hissed. 'Look what's stuck on the wall over there!'

Right above the payment desk near the door was a grainy close-up poster of yours truly.

It was a bigger version of the ones I'd seen in another internet café a while back.

'Let's get out of here,' I said.

'I'll go and pay the guy,' whispered Boges. 'You'd better just walk out. I'll meet you near the clock tower.'

6:20 pm

I didn't have to hang around the clock tower for very long before I saw Boges puffing his way towards me. I was getting skinnier by the day while he was getting rounder.

'Do you think he recognised me?' I asked when Boges pulled up beside me.

'Not sure, dude. But it's definitely time for you to get out of town. And this time I mean it!'

We both started walking through a light drizzle, heading for the highway and the chance of a ride for me. The traffic was slow because of the rain but all the time I was looking over my shoulder, scared that I'd see a black Subaru, or a dark blue Mercedes.

While walking towards the highway, Boges and I talked through ideas about how we could find out more information to help us solve the DMO.

'I don't even know if Jennifer Smith has tried to get in touch with me,' I said, 'since I lost my other phone.'

'That sucks,' Boges puffed. 'There's gotta be important information on your dad's memory stick. Maybe I'll try her at Labtech. If she's not there any more, they might be able to give me a forwarding address or something.'

It was good to know that Boges was on the job just like I was. I remembered the odd incident Jennifer had told me about—my dad asking for the book *Treasure Island* and throwing it on the floor when the nurse gave a copy to him. Even though I didn't expect any amazing insight, I told Boges about it.

'I don't know what to make of that,' said Boges. 'He was pretty sick by then, wasn't he? Probably just confused. What about that Eric guy who worked with your dad? Could you try once more to get in touch with him?'

'Yep, I can try him at Dad's old work again. That shouldn't be too hard.'

'Let's hope your great-uncle in the country will be able to help us with more information,' said Boges. 'On the Singularity, the Riddle, the drawings. Anything he knows would be good. That's if you get there without the cops picking you up first.'

Eager to get to Great-uncle Bartholomew's as soon as I could, I picked up the pace, jogging towards the highway.

6:37 pm

Boges was getting tired so we slowed down and walked the few remaining blocks to the highway.

'You haven't had much luck hitching rides, Cal,' Boges said as he panted along beside me. 'You sure you want to try it again?'

'Don't know if I have much choice. Hopefully all my bad luck's out of the way,' I said with a nervous laugh.

Boges gave me one of his bear hugs, then whacked me on the back, farewelling me.

'Stay outta trouble, now, will ya?' he laughed. Now he was the one who sounded nervous. 'I'll keep researching what I can, and message you if I find out anything. Keep in touch, OK. Don't leave me hanging.'

20 MAY

226 days to go . . .

2:38 pm

I stood in the rain, sodden and cold, trying to work out what move to make next. There'd been such a massive downpour after Boges left me yesterday that I had to abandon my hitchhiking plans and run from the road to find shelter for the night. I ended up sleeping huddled in the fire stairs of an old apartment block, trying to ignore the fact that it stank like a toilet.

This morning I jumped on a bus that was going straight up the highway, and was taken at least a couple of hours closer to where I wanted to be. I hopped off just after it turned onto a major exit, and I'd been wandering along near the highway, in the cold drizzle, ever since.

I was so glad that Dad's drawings and the Ormond Riddle were safe in their plastic folder in my new backpack. Boges had also collected the guardian angel pin that Repro had given me, and I'd pinned it near the neck of my T-shirt, just under my hoodie. Repro said it had helped him—I figured it might help me finally find my way to Mount Helicon. So far it had brought me the bus, which had saved me hours and hours of walking.

The drizzle was becoming heavier. I didn't know if anyone on the road could even see me, but they definitely weren't interested in slowing down to offer me a ride.

6:51 pm

The weather had eased up, but now night had settled in. I was already looking for somewhere to camp, counting on hitching a ride the rest of the way in the morning.

A strange feeling of déjà vu suddenly came over me.

I started recognising where I was. I remembered this place. I'd been here before.

Melba Snipe's house
Valley Heights

7:38 pm

'Tom!' Melba cried happily, when she peered through her screen door and realised it was me shivering there.

'Mrs Snipe!' I said, just as happy to see her kind face.

'Come in, come in! My goodness you look like a drowned rat! Sit down, dear. Let me grab you a blanket and a cuppa.'

I was back in the old floral house with its green-tinted walls and proud picture frames, and it felt good. Timmy, the yappy little dog, came flying down the hallway to see what was going on.

'Here,' said Melba, returning from the closet with a big, woollen blanket. She draped it over me. 'Oh, get down, Timmy,' she said, brushing the wild ball of fur away. 'I've been thinking of you, Tom, ever since you left here that day—whatever happened with your poor little sister?'

'She's OK. I saw her in the hospital,' I said, casting my mind back to the hellish journey I had made to get to Gabbi before they switched off her life support. 'I got there just in time to see her show some signs of improvement. She's still not out of the woods, but I think she's on her way.'

'Oh, thank goodness. That's wonderful to hear, really wonderful. So, Tom, what brings you around here again?'

I quickly thought back to minutes ago when

I'd played out this conversation in my head, planning what I would say to Melba to explain my sudden arrival.

'I'm on my way to visit my uncle,' I said, 'and I know it's late, but I thought I'd stop by and say hello and let you know that I dropped that book off to your friend Elvira's letterbox, back in the city, a few weeks ago.' I paused, slightly nervous about asking for a favour from this kind-hearted woman. 'Would it be OK if I stayed here for the night? I'll be off again early in the morning.'

'Of course!' Melba beamed. 'You can have the couch again, if you don't mind it! I'll put the kettle on and look in my son's old things again for some dry clothes. Make yourself comfortable. And Timmy,' she waved a finger at her pet, 'you leave Cal alone!'

Cal? Did she just call me Cal?! My heart started racing as the old woman hummed away to herself in the kitchen, then wandered down the hallway to fetch some of her son's clothes. Did she know who I was? I was pretty sure I heard her right!

'Here,' she said, passing me an old grey tracksuit top and pants. They had three white stripes down the sides, and were clean, but smelled like they'd been in storage for years. 'These should fit you.'

'Thanks,' I said tentatively, placing them beside me on the couch.

She poured us some tea in the kitchen, and then brought it out on a tray. I took mine and let the cup warm my hands.

'Mrs Snipe?' I asked.

'Yes, dear?'

'You just called me "Cal".'

She gasped, bringing her frail hand to her mouth.

'Oops,' she said, before moving her hand to my knee. 'So I did. Love, in spite of my age, and my forgetfulness,' she continued with a bit of a cheeky grin, 'I do realise who you are. It wasn't too hard to put two and two together since you were last here. But you have nothing to worry about, you have my word. I'm not interested in dobbing you in.'

'Really?' I asked, shocked and pretty embarrassed that I'd just assumed she had no idea. I should have realised when she invited me into her house after finding me hiding out in the boot of her car, last month, that she was no ordinary old lady.

She looked deep into my eyes and nodded sincerely. 'Promise. I don't believe the reports,' she said with a sweeping wave of her arms. 'I know you're not capable of such savagery . . .

and unfortunately I know very well how a boy's luck, and maybe a couple of bad decisions, can send his life into a spin. It's just important that one day you gain control again.'

I nodded back, appreciatively.

'I think it will happen for you, Cal. You're such a clever boy, and you have a kind heart, I can feel it. Oh—' she said, the serious tone of her voice suddenly changing to one of surprise, 'I used to have one just like that,' she said, tapping the guardian angel pin on my T-shirt.

She sat back again—a teary glaze washed over her eyes. 'Anyway, not to worry, OK? You should clean up and get some rest.'

21 MAY

225 days to go . . .

1:52 pm

I left sweet, old Melba Snipe a little while after breakfast, and promised her I'd be back to visit another time.

I really hoped I would see her again—I felt strangely connected to her. I still couldn't get over how she knew who I was, but was OK with it. If only everyone else could be that trusting of me.

The rain had stopped as I walked alongside the highway, but evidence of the downpour was everywhere. My sneakers were soaked from the puddles.

2:46 pm

Gratefully, I hopped into a van that had slowed down for me, after jumping back so that it wouldn't spray me with water. The driver, a middle-aged guy with a cattle dog in the back, introduced himself as Brian, and the dog as Dodger, before asking my name.

'I'm Ben,' I said, in answer to his question, hoping that this Ben Galloway ID wouldn't cause me any problems. I stowed my backpack on the floor while the dog sniffed my neck.

'Where are you headed?'

'Mount Helicon.'

'You're in luck. My place isn't far from there.'

Brian was a CB radio fan, and the minute I got in and closed the door he took off, continuing the radio chat that had been interrupted when he stopped to pick me up.

From the boxes in the back, and the oranges and lemons on the floor, I gathered that he had an orchard or some other sort of citrus farm. He certainly had the leathery look of a man who spends most of his days outside in the sun and wind. His skin was almost the same colour as his brown hair.

Being in Brian's van reminded me of my ride with Lachlan. I hoped there wasn't going to be a repeat of the tailgating nightmare. Anxiously, I looked behind us, but all was clear.

Brian was fiddling with his CB radio, changing bands and channels, muttering to himself. 'Don't know what's the matter with this thing. There's some local interference. You haven't got some program running, have you?'

'Me?' I asked, surprised. 'I haven't got anything electrical running. My mobile's not even switched on.'

'Well the darn thing is playing up for some reason,' he said, switching it off. 'Maybe there's a UFO nearby!' he joked.

4:27 pm

'Now what's this all about?' said Brian, slowing down.

I looked ahead and immediately clenched in fear. Halfway across the road, a police car was parked and an officer was waving us down with a glowing red baton. I tried to relax, remembering I had fake ID now, hoping it would stand up to scrutiny. I also hoped that Sligo didn't have the authorities looking for Ben Galloway, although I didn't think that was likely—I'd be no use to him locked up and out of his reach.

The police officer was waving us down and our car stopped completely.

The cop stood back and squinted hard at both of us through the window. Finally, he strolled around to my side while I sat trying to look relaxed and curious.

'What's the problem, officer?' asked Brian.

'No problem for you,' he said. 'It's your passenger I'm interested in. Got any ID, son?'

I fumbled in my backpack and finally pulled out the Ben Galloway bus pass. 'I've got my bus pass,' I said, as casually as possible.

I passed it to him and he checked it out, glancing from my photo to me.

'Hang on a minute. I need to check this out.'

4:39 pm

It seemed to take forever for him to return from his patrol car.

'What's he doing?' I asked Brian, hoping that I sounded like any interested teenager.

'He'd just be checking your name against the police records,' he said dismissively.

Eventually, the police officer returned and handed me my bus pass. 'OK, driver,' he said, looking already to the car that had pulled up behind us. 'On your way.'

4:55 pm

Brian turned to me. 'What are you going to do in Mount Helicon?'

'I'm hoping to get a job on one of the properties there,' I said.

'What's the name of it? I know most of the people there.'

I risked giving away too much information if I told the truth, but if I lied, chances were that Brian would become suspicious, especially if he knew most people in the area.

'You probably wouldn't know it. It's some way out of town.'

'Try me,' he challenged, 'I bet I do know.'

I knew I couldn't make anything up now.

'It's called "Kilkenny".'

Brian swung round to face me, looking surprised. 'Old Barty's place? No way!'

'Why?' I asked, starting to get worried.

'Oh boy, you don't know? The old guy's absolutely bonkers. He carries a shotgun and takes a pot shot at anybody who comes onto his property.'

'Anybody?'

'*Everybody*,' corrected Brian. 'I'd be careful going near the crazy old guy if I were you! Anyway, not far to go now,' he said, as we swung around the Mount Helicon turnoff. 'Hopefully he won't shoot at you!'

'Kilkenny'
Mount Helicon

6:09 pm

I stood on the roadside, shivering. I zipped up

my tracksuit top, and hitched up my backpack. The sky behind the tall trees along the horizon was glowing with sunset, and for a second it seemed like a warning.

Brian's tail-lights slowly vanished in the distance, and I wondered what I was in for next. I really didn't want to be greeted with a gun.

I swung the long, country-style gates open, closed them behind me and started walking up the long driveway, towards the house, which I could just see behind a mass of dark trees.

As I got closer, I wondered whether I should yell out first, so that Great-uncle Bartholomew knew that I was his nephew, or whether I should go right up to the door and call out from there.

I was still trying to make up my mind when something swooped down on me from the trees. I jumped back in fright, waving my arms around my head to fight whatever it was off me. But it happened again. A sharp beak and claws scraped my hair—it was a big bird of some sort! I fought it off again, waiting to see if it would attack again.

I didn't know where it had gone so I cautiously stepped onto the verandah. Things didn't look very promising. Great-uncle Bartholomew's house was in darkness and seemed to be defended by some vigilant attack bird. I couldn't see any lights coming from the windows. Maybe it was deserted, I thought. Great-uncle Bartholomew might even be dead.

The night wind rustled in the trees near the house, spooking me. With a deep breath, I took a step forward and knocked on the door.

'Uncle Bartholomew!' I called in what I hoped was a strong and friendly voice.

I waited. Someone stirred inside; he wasn't dead.

'Bartholomew?' I called again.

'Get off my property! If you don't leave in one second, I'll shoot! I've got two barrels loaded, so if I miss you the first time I'll get you the next!'

I jumped back from the front door. *He* mightn't be dead, but if I didn't convince him to put the gun down, I could be!

'Don't shoot! It's me! Cal! Your nephew! Tom's son! I need to talk to you!'

A huge explosion sounded inside and I stumbled back off the verandah, tripping over into a bush. The deranged old man had fired the shotgun!

'I warned you! Get off my land or I'll shoot again!'

My eardrums were deafened from the sound of the shotgun. I lay back in the bush, dazed, ears thick with throbbing. The fear inside me quickly faded, and was replaced with red-hot anger. I'd been through hell trying to get to this place. I wasn't going to let him scare me off! Or kill me!

'Listen here!' I yelled. 'I'm your *nephew!* I'm Cal! Cal Ormond!'

I struggled to get back on my feet.

'People have been trying to get rid of me for months!' I continued yelling. 'I've been kid-napped! I've escaped drowning, being flattened by a train, a psychiatric asylum . . . I've been on the run for almost five months, and I've come here hoping that you'd be the one person left in my family that could help me out of this night-mare! So if you're determined to shoot your own nephew, go ahead! It wouldn't be the first time I've been shot at! I'm innocent, and I need help! I'm not leaving until you've told me what you know about the Ormond Singularity and the Ormond Riddle!'

I waited, on my feet now, tensing up for the next shot.

But nothing happened.

I stood in the dark, waiting.

I was about to start yelling again when I heard the front door rattle. I braced myself.

After a number of bolts were released the

front door opened just enough for Great-uncle Bartholomew to stick his nose through.

'Did I hear you say "Ormond Riddle"?'

'That's what I said.'

'And did you say "Ormond Singularity"?'

'I did.'

'You're Winifred and Tom's son?'

'That's right.'

Another pause.

'You're Callum?'

'That's me.'

The door creaked open wider.

'So it is! It *is* you! You've changed quite a bit since I saw you last. You're just like Tom was at your age!' Bartholomew said, slowly stepping out to look at me. He ran his flashlight over me. I stared at the shotgun in his other arm.

'Sorry about that,' he said, shakily putting the gun down against the wall. 'You've got to protect yourself around here, especially when you're as old as I am.'

I tried to smile back, but it was hard to forget that this grinning old guy in front of me was taking shots at me just seconds ago.

'Welcome to "Kilkenny",' he said pulling his saggy trousers up. 'I was just on my way to check the Ormond Orca. Come with me and let's get acquainted.'

Ormond Orca? What else was there that carried my family's name?

'The Orca's been my life's work,' he said, switching on a powerful light that was angled to shine on a large shed to the left of the house.

I cautiously followed my unusual relative, and took a good look at him. He wore an ancient leather jacket lined with wool, over a slightly moth-eaten jumper. I half expected him to have flying goggles on his head but, instead, a bright red woollen beanie was pulled down low over his ears, matched by a red-check scarf tied jauntily around his neck. He looked like he hadn't shaved for several days—white bristles poked out in patches around his jaw. His face was lined and wrinkled, but his eyes twinkled behind a pair of bifocal glasses.

'Sounds like you've been having a rough time lately,' he said, referring to my earlier outburst.

'You could say that. I'm surprised you haven't been following it in the news.'

'I don't pay much attention to the news these days,' he said as we crunched through the gravel towards the big shed. 'I don't care for TV or newspapers, I only listen to my transistor radio. I'm too old and my time is too precious to worry any more about what's going on beyond my gates. Here, give us a hand with the door. I check the Orca every day, do a walk-around. It's an essential part of aviation safety.'

We pushed the door open, and a floodlight filled the room.

I gasped in surprise. A streamlined aeroplane, black and white, gleamed, every line of it seeming to reach forwards and upwards, as if it was straining on a leash, just dying to be let off. Towards the end of the aircraft, sitting down the back and framed by the V-shaped tail fins behind it, was the distinctive elongated egg-shape of a jet engine.

'Wicked!' I said, already forgetting for a moment that I had just narrowly avoided being shot by this wild old man. 'You've built a jet!'

My stunned surprise pleased my uncle as he walked proudly around the beautiful craft.

'Hey,' I said, 'cool registration—52-ORC. Oscar, Romeo, Charlie,' I quoted, remembering what I'd learned as an air cadet.

The eccentric aviator smiled and patted me on the back. 'Yes, I was lucky to get those letters.'

Ahead of the Ormond Orca was another set of double doors, which opened wide onto a vast paddock. I could just make out the shadows of the distant hills beyond.

'So, what do you think?' he said, digging his

hands into his trouser pockets. 'Built it myself. My own private jet. Pretty well designed the launching system, too. The RATO.'

'RATO?'

'Rocket Assisted Take-Off,' said my uncle, patting a sleek cylinder underneath the aeroplane's body, and above the wheel housings. 'Takes a while for a jet like this to warm up. If you want to get away OK, you need some help, that's why the front doors of the shed are always open, ready for take-off.'

'Unreal!' I said, turning to him with respect. 'I'm learning to fly,' I said, then corrected myself. 'I *was* learning to fly, until Dad got sick. But I've only flown regular small aeroplanes, and paragliders, nothing like this. Not a jet!'

'You're your father's son all right. Tom was crazy about flying.'

Outside, the wind rose, whistling through the cracks in the big shed, filling the sad silence that followed my uncle's words.

My great-uncle began his inspection of the Orca, walking around its sleek length, carefully examining it with the help of a powerful flashlight, squatting and peering to look under it, checking the rocket cylinders, and lastly climbing up onto the wing to check the canopy. I followed closely.

'I kept the console as straightforward as possible,' said Bartholomew, as I peered inside the cabin to see the dials that were familiar to me—the control yoke, the floating compass indicating north, south, east and west, the two large levers of the throttles in the centre of the console, the altitude indicator with its artificial horizon, and the airspeed indicator, like the speedometer in a car.

I jumped down and my uncle clambered back to the ground slowly and carefully, grunting with the effort.

'Some people lock up the chickens every night, or tuck the kids in . . . but I check the aeroplane,' he said, his face lighting up with a grin. He put the torch back on the shelf and closed the door of the hangar-like shed.

'So you still fly?' I asked, as I followed him back to the house.

'Not for a long time now. I've got a dicky ticker—a lousy heart—and just in case I need urgent help, I keep the aeroplane here, so that I can be flown to the nearest intensive care. Plenty of fuel in the tanks. There's a chap in town who's agreed to act as my safety pilot, for when I finally take the jet out. They reckon I'm too old to go up alone.'

6:49 pm

Back on the verandah, the old man picked up the shotgun he'd left propped on the wall, and carried it broken open over his arm.

'Sorry about the reception I gave you,' he said. 'There's no shot in these cartridges. They're just for show. Or rather, for the noise they make. Not like the chap on the next lot. He uses live shot. But that's another story. Speaking of stories, I think we need to settle down with a drink and hear yours.'

7:02 pm

Once inside the house I understood, as we walked down the narrow hallway and into the large room at the end of it, why I hadn't seen any lights from the driveway. The space was lit with kerosene lamps and candles that cast nothing but a soft glow, leaving much of the place in deep shadow.

I paused for a moment, looking up at the ceiling and furniture with amazement. Dad always said that Great-uncle Bartholomew was an eccentric aviator—and he hadn't been wrong. And it wasn't just because he'd built his own jet. His place was like a workshop and flight museum. There were bits of aeroplane everywhere, but they weren't all being worked on: some parts he'd turned into furnishings!

A four-bladed propeller, holding four flickering candles, hung low in the living room like a massive candelabra. Melted wax stalactites dropped from it, some of them dripping down onto the threadbare carpet, where they formed an equally big X-shape. The walls held pictures and posters of old-fashioned planes, while the shelves carried volumes of flying magazines and journals. Sections of aeroplane instrument panels, old sextants and other navigational instruments were scattered around haphazardly. In one corner, an entire aircraft engine block, sitting on bricks with a big cushion on it, formed a sort of chair. What looked like most of a cockpit and part of the fuselage of some World War II warbird was pulled up next to a long bench-like table that was made out of the wing of another aircraft. I guessed this must have been like his desk, judging by the papers, pens and empty coffee mug sitting on it.

Just beyond this, alone on the top of an antique wooden sideboard, shone a scale model of the Ormond Orca, complete with small rockets on each side of its undercarriage.

Bartholomew, seeing my interest in the model, came up beside me. 'You should see the way the launching system works. All it needs is a little rocket fuel. It can do an almost vertical take-off.'

He put his hands on my shoulders, turning my face into the light that shone from the candles flickering along the propeller blades.

'Tom's son, eh? Then let's have a good look at you. Haven't seen you since you were a tiny little chap no higher than my flying boots. How old are you, Cal?'

'I'll be sixteen in a couple of months,' I said. Sadness washed over me as I realised that in a couple of months my dad would have been dead for a whole year. In July—the same month as my birthday.

Great-uncle Bartholomew studied me for a while and nodded. 'Yes, I can see your father in those eyes, God rest his soul.'

He sat himself down again, his bottom lip quivering.

'Makes me wish I'd seen more of my family, especially now that Tom's gone. I'm sure it doesn't seem like it, with me living out here on my own and all, but I do realise that family and friendships are the important things.'

'Yeah,' I agreed. 'I don't know what I would have done without my mate Boges. Or the thought of one day being happy with Mum and Gabbi again.'

'You've had to grow up quickly, Cal. You've got an old head on young shoulders—that's what we used to say about people like you. Now you need to—'

Bartholomew was cut short by a strange whirring sound and movement from above that made me duck for cover. It was a large magpie! It had suddenly flown in from upstairs, circled the room and then flapped over to the aircraft engine block. It was the attack bird!

'That's the bird that had a go at me earlier,' I said, 'when I was walking up to the house. It dive-bombed me!'

'Oh, Maggers,' chuckled my great-uncle, almost with as much pride in his voice as he had when he spoke about the Orca. 'He's a fighter pilot. Soon as he sees an intruder, he dives for them!'

The large black and white bird folded his wings and looked at me with his brown eyes gleaming in the firelight.

'I painted my jet in his colours,' said my great-uncle, 'but on that aircraft, the black and white reminded me more of a killer whale than a magpie and that's why I called it the Ormond Orca. What's got into you, you funny bird?' he said, as he stroked the magpie's feathers. 'Why aren't you asleep? It's past your bedtime.'

Maggers half closed his eyes while my uncle ruffled the feathers around his neck. The magpie then made a soft, carolling sound and flew up into the high corners of the room and perched in the shadows.

'I found him on the ground after a storm. Hand-raised him. He's a great companion. Doesn't even mind the sound of the shotgun.'

I was aware of the rustling as Maggers resettled himself, roosting for the night.

Once we'd settled down at the aircraft-wing table, my great-uncle lit another kerosene lamp, cut some bread and cheese and poured some tea. 'Now, over to you and your story,' he prompted.

I hesitated. He said he didn't care for the news, so I had no idea how much he knew or didn't know. I couldn't see a TV anywhere, although I could hear dull voices on a radio somewhere, intermittently jammed by bad static.

'Where to begin . . .' I sighed.

I started with Dad's trip to Ireland and the letter he'd written to me from there, hinting at a massive secret and warning me of danger. I continued with Dad's illness, the drawings he'd made before he died, and then, well, his death . . . which led into a detailed recollection of the series of terrible events that had happened to me and my family since then. Once I'd told him about the attack at home that left Gabbi in intensive care, I found it was easy to keep going.

It was an unbelievable feeling to be able to talk to him, without holding back—someone who was family, the younger brother of my late Ormond grandfather. Bartholomew listened without interruption until I was finished—and so were the bread and the cheese.

22 MAY

224 days to go . . .

9:04 am

📱 made it 2 mount helicon. all cool. awesome place. making progress. b in touch again soon.

10:19 am

After our massive talk last night, Great-uncle Bartholomew set me up on an air mattress in a room occupied only by an old-fashioned dressing table and mirror. I could see that I'd had him up much later than he was used to— he looked exhausted, and his age was really showing—and I had a sore throat from talking so much.

We'd met up again at the wing table over a lazy breakfast of sausages and tomatoes.

'You *have* had a time of it, haven't you,' he said, with a messy mouthful of sausage. 'I listen to the radio sometimes, and I did hear something about a youngster with the Ormond name who was in strife. I wondered about you, especially after getting Tom's letter.'

'You got a letter from Dad?'

'Sure I did,' he said, slopping barbecue sauce awkwardly over his plate. 'I called your mother a few times after Tom's funeral, explaining why I couldn't go. The dicky ticker was playing up. I think I even called her sometime earlier this year—I'm pretty sure it was after I heard the name Ormond on the radio, but I wouldn't bet on it—and I must say that she sounded quite strange . . .'

'She'd been through a lot.'

'I was a bit worried about her. I called back a little later, but the phone had been disconnected.'

'Yeah, she moved into Rafe's place. Actually, it's her place now. Rafe signed it over to her.'

'That's generous,' said my great-uncle, his bushy, white eyebrows rising.

'You said Dad had written to you,' I reminded him.

'Yes, yes, so he did. Not quite sure where his letter is right now, but he told me he'd stumbled upon the Ormond Angel and the rumours of a great secret to do with the family from hundreds of years ago. He wanted to come and see me—he'd remembered I had some old documents stored here somewhere, related to the family. I warned him I didn't know if I could help him, but I used to have some information about Piers Ormond's will. When you get to my age, you can't help becoming a bit of an archivist. An archivist who can't remember what he has!'

This was more information than I'd had in ages. I felt a thrill of excitement rush over me. 'And do you? Do you have information about Piers Ormond's will?'

'Possibly,' said Great-uncle Bartholomew, sounding very unsure. 'I'd have to look through all my papers.'

'There's a *lot* of paper here,' I said, twisting around to look at the room.

'It'll be around here somewhere.'

The library of journals and magazines, and the amazing collection of aircraft parts, reminded me of Repro's place.

'What about the Ormond Singularity?' I asked, turning back to him. 'Do you know anything about it?'

'The Ormond Singularity. Now that's a familiar phrase,' he said, frowning, 'but I haven't heard of it for many, many years. I think I've forgotten what it was all about—if I ever knew.'

'But you *have* heard of it,' I said. 'And what about the Ormond Riddle?'

'Most definitely—the Ormond Riddle,' he said,

nodding. 'Yes, yes. The Ormond family is full of secrets. It's just that I've forgotten most of them.'

I knew it was up to me to jog the old man's memory. I dug around in my backpack and brought out the plastic folder with the drawings, the transparency with the names written on it and the soft vellum fabric of the Ormond Riddle. My great-uncle picked this up with reverent hands.

'I don't believe my eyes!' he exclaimed. 'Where did you get this? This looks like the original manuscript! I didn't think *this* was what you stole from that Oriana de la whatever's place! You did well, boy! I heard the Riddle had disappeared during my grandfather's time. Until it was stolen, it had always been in the family, handed down from generation to generation. I don't know where that woman got it from, but collectors love this sort of thing. There's a big trade in antiquities like this.'

Great-uncle Bartholomew must have been well over eighty, so something that happened in *his* grandfather's time was a long time ago. I did a fast and rough calculation, wishing that Boges—the handy human calculator—was around. I figured the theft must have taken place back in the 1850s—over a hundred and fifty years ago.

I watched while the old man read over the fancy writing of the Riddle a couple of times.

The ORMOND RIDDLE

Eight are the Leaves on my Ladyes Grace

Fayre sits the Rounde of my Ladyes Face

Thirteen Teares from the Sunnes grate Doore

Make right to treadde in Gules on the Floore

But adde One in for the Queenes fayre Sinne

Then alle shall be tolde and the Yifte unfold

Finally, he looked up. 'I'd heard it was a difficult riddle,' he said, 'especially with the last two lines missing.'

'You knew about that?'

'Oh yes. The Riddle was damaged—sabotaged—centuries ago. Someone cut off the last two lines in the eighteenth century or even earlier, probably out of spite, so it would be near impossible to solve. There is no lack of spite in the world.'

Carefully, he put the vellum back down on the wing table, frowning. 'What is creating that interference with my weather channel?' he said, looking around, crankily. 'That darn static!'

I wished he'd just turn the crackling radio off. It had been spluttering for a few minutes now.

'It's a great adventure you've got yourself into, Cal,' he continued. 'And I'm glad it's not too late for me to get to know you, and help you in any way I can. You're more than welcome to hide out here for as long as you like. It's no Taj Mahal, but it's no Leechwood Lodge, either. No straitjackets, I promise!'

It was great to have him on my side. Melba had been another surprising source of kindness, but it was even better to have a relative backing me up. The rest of my family were in no position to help.

'Thanks, Uncle,' I said, over the static on the radio.

He stood up and patted me on the shoulder, before walking over to his radio, trying to fix the tuning.

'I like listening to the weather channel,' he said. 'It reminds me of my flying days. All the briefings about the weather and flying restrictions for pilots—got a little generator that keeps me running. There,' he said, turning back to me. 'I think that sounds a little better. Now where were we? Yes, the Ormond Riddle. Some people say that it is no more than a nonsense rhyme, others say that it's a very valuable part of history and a big secret.'

'I have a friend,' I started to say, thinking of Winter, 'and she's suggested that it's a number riddle.'

'Could be, could be,' my great-uncle nodded. 'Who knows . . . Either way, it *is* the Ormond Riddle and I'm glad it's back in the family again.'

He looked up, frowning, distracted again by the rhythmic static that was once more cutting into his radio channel. 'I'm damned if I know what that interference is all about. I don't know what's wrong with it!'

Funny, I thought. Brian had mentioned interference too on his CB radio, before joking about UFOs. Maybe it was the weather.

Great-uncle Bartholomew switched his attention over to the drawings, which I'd laid out along the wing table.

'My dad drew this Angel twice as you can see,' I said, 'and it led us to the stained glass window at Memorial Park—in memory of Piers Ormond.'

'He died before my time. But what about all these other drawings? Did Tom do all of them?'

'Yeah. Boges and I have been trying to decipher them ever since I got them. Uncle Rafe tried to hide them from me, when they first arrived, even though they were addressed to me.'

'Rafe is an interesting chap,' said my uncle. 'Perhaps he was trying to protect you, keep you from getting upset. I must say I was happily surprised to hear from you that he'd signed over his house to Win.'

'Me too.'

Bartholomew pushed himself up from the table, and onto his feet. 'Wanna come work on the Orca with me?'

30 MAY

216 days to go ...

6:25 pm

It was nearing the end of another almost-blissful day of working on the Orca and getting to know my great-uncle. I'd been at his place for over a week now, and in a strange way I was happy that my life on the run had taken me to him.

Bartholomew put his tools down and rubbed his hands together. 'It's getting pretty cold in here. Let's head back inside and have another look at those drawings. I'll stir up the fire and heat us up something to eat.'

'Sounds good to me,' I agreed.

6:34 pm

My uncle heaved an engine part aside to reveal a pile of kindling and split timber. He placed it across the glowing coals, and soon a brighter and more cheerful blaze lit the room, sending dark shadows jumping and dancing on the walls and ceiling.

He turned to the drawings again, but couldn't concentrate. 'That darn static,' he said, leaving the room and calling back, 'I'm going to have to switch the radio off!'

I went over to the fire and warmed myself, waiting for him to come back, and waiting for the leftover potato and leek soup from the night before to heat up. He returned with a puzzled look on his face.

'That interference, it's local interference. And I don't understand where it could possibly be coming from. I certainly don't have anything running here. Are you running some sort of electronic gadget in that backpack of yours? You youngsters have all sorts of fancy whiz-bangs these days.'

Brian with the CB radio had asked me the same question.

'No whiz-bangs on me,' I said. My phone wasn't even switched on.

'I don't understand,' he said, scratching slowly at his white stubble. Without the chatter and buzz of the radio, things were quiet now. All we could hear was the crackling of the fire. He shook his head, and peered down at the drawings.

'So what have you and your friends worked out so far?' he asked, changing the subject.

'We think we've solved a couple of them,' I said, telling him about the things that can be worn.

'But of course it can be worn!' exclaimed my great-uncle energetically.

'What can be worn?' I said, not knowing what he was talking about. 'What do you mean?'

Great-uncle Bartholomew looked at me as if I were stupid. 'There's no mystery. That's what jewels are for, aren't they? To be worn?'

'Sorry, what jewels are we talking about here?'

My eccentric relative blinked slowly before speaking very clearly. 'The Ormond Jewel!' he said, tasting the soup.

I was speechless. *The Ormond Jewel*? Sligo drilled me about a jewel, back at the car yard!

'The Ormond Jewel,' Great-uncle Bartholomew repeated. 'That's obviously what the drawing means. Something that can be worn. And look there,' he pointed to the Ormond Angel's chest, 'the Ormond Angel is wearing it in both drawings.'

I stared hard at where he was pointing, and was able to make out something that could have been some kind of jewel in each of the drawings, but I wasn't so sure about that.

'Mind you,' my uncle said, 'I've always thought that the Ormond Jewel was just another family legend—or that if it did exist, it would have vanished years ago, been broken up and sold on, probably centuries ago. But I thought you would have heard of it, if you have heard of the Ormond Riddle. They go together like a horse and cart.'

First there had been an Ormond Angel, then an Ormond Riddle, then the Ormond Singularity and now, Bartholomew was talking about the Ormond Jewel! That went together with the Riddle, like a horse and cart!

'We suspected something had been taken from the empty jewellery box we found in Dad's suitcase, after the break-in back home in Richmond,' I said, starting to feel convinced that the Ormond Jewel must have once been in Dad's possession. 'What else do you know about it?'

My great-uncle wasn't paying attention to me. Instead, he was standing perfectly still, head cocked to one side, listening intently. 'There's someone out there,' he said. 'I can hear a car. I can hear cars that are kilometres away. Where's my shotgun?'

'Please,' I said, 'tell me about the Ormond Jewel. I think Dad might have got hold of it. I think he had it in his suitcase.'

But Great-uncle Bartholomew wasn't in the

mood for discussions about a missing jewel. He was busy loading two cartridges into the barrel of his shotgun. With the gun broken over his arm, he headed upstairs. I was frustrated that he'd been so easily distracted and quick to get his gun out, just because he heard some car in the distance. At this stage, *nothing* could be more important than getting information about the Ormond Jewel. I would have to tell Boges about it!

From the shadows near the ceiling, Maggers made a strange, menacing warning call. My excitement fell away, replaced by fear. What if the car that my great-uncle had heard contained people who were trying to get hold of everything of mine that was spread on the wing table?

Now, the jumping shadows thrown into dark corners by the fire seemed ugly and dangerous, and the occasional crackles and small explosions sounded like the snapping of twigs beneath a predator's stealthy steps.

I hurried up the stairs in the direction my great-uncle had taken, my heart pounding.

The second floor also housed aeroplane parts and shrouded shapes under drop cloths. I imagined crouching dangers lurking underneath as I hurried after Bartholomew. I found him in the room that overlooked the front of his property, squinting through a telescope that was mounted in the window. He adjusted it, moving it a little to the left or right while squinting down the lens.

He jumped back then shouted in triumph. 'I told you! There's someone driving back and forth along the road that runs past my property. Take a look for yourself!'

Sure enough, I could see a vehicle through the lens. As moonlight passed over it, I realised it was the dark blue Mercedes!

How had Oriana followed me here?

'It's them!' I screeched to my uncle, my eyes flickering around to check out the top of the stairs behind him, as if the enemy were already inside the house. 'That car belongs to Oriana de la Force!'

'Those scoundrels had better not step a foot on my land!' said Great-uncle Bartholomew, 'or I'll load them up with bird shot!' Then he turned to me, grabbing both of my shoulders. 'But how did they know you were here? How could they?'

'I don't know! They must have followed me! They always seem to be able to track me down!'

'But you hitchhiked. How would they know which car you were in?'

'I don't know,' I repeated. 'And that was days ago, anyway!'

'Somehow, they've been able to make a bee-line for you. It's as if they've got you fair and square on their radar screen.'

'But that couldn't be, unless . . .' my voice trailed off. I remembered the interference on Brian's CB radio. And the rhythmic static that had ruined the weather broadcasts on Great-uncle Bartholomew's radio. A crazy idea came to my mind. My great-uncle took the words out of my mouth.

'Unless *you're* transmitting something,' he said, wide-eyed.

'If I'm transmitting something, it means I've been—'

'Bugged! They've bloomin' well bugged you, my boy!'

6:56 pm

I raced downstairs, shoved all my stuff into my backpack, and hauled it upstairs again.

'I'm going to check everything I own,' I called out on my way to the bathroom.

He nodded vigorously, bringing me a kerosene lamp.

I plugged the bathtub and began tipping the contents of my bag into it. Swiftly, I examined everything I owned and then the backpack itself, running my fingers into every nook and cranny.

I wasn't sure what I was looking for. I'd never seen a bug before but I imagined it would be pretty small.

Next I pulled off the clothes I was wearing and checked them. They were a big zero—I didn't find anything and anyway, *Boges* had given me those. Boges had given me the new backpack, too. It would have been impossible for anyone to bug any of my things. And yet, somehow the blue Mercedes was out on the road, just a kilometre or so away. I got dressed again, and as I yanked the hoodie over my head, I knocked the sore spot on my right shoulder into a hook on the wall. I swore.

'Are you all right?' my great-uncle called from the doorway. 'Did you find it?'

'I couldn't find anything,' I said. What if they were using some state-of-the-art nano bug, as small as a grain of sand?

'What's that blood on your shoulder?'

'What blood?' I asked, trying to pull my hoodie to one side, and craning my neck to see what he was talking about.

A growing blood patch stained the fabric over my right shoulder.

'I'd better have a look at that. Hurry and come down where there's more light,' suggested Bartholomew. 'Looks like you've got a boil or some nasty infection there,' he said shining his powerful flashlight over me. 'A carbuncle.'

'A carbuncle?'

'I think I should put some antiseptic on it. You must have knocked it, or it's come to a head. Something's happened to make it bleed.'

'I just bumped it on the towel hook. Whatever you have to do, make it quick!'

While I gingerly felt around the back of my shoulder, pressing the swelling and the hot, infected skin with my fingertips, Bartholomew foraged through a little basket and pulled out some cotton wool and a small bottle, the contents of which he dabbed on my shoulder.

'Yee-ow!' I flinched. 'Take it easy. What's that? Sulphuric acid?!'

Bartholomew had already stopped dabbing. He was peering intently at the infection. 'I don't like the look of this at all. It looks like you've got something under your skin.'

'Maybe the spot where I was jabbed with the tranquilliser has become infected?'

'Can't be. This is nowhere near your neck. This looks nasty. There's pus and blood oozing everywhere.' He dabbed it again until I jerked away when he hit the really sore spot.

As I did this, Bartholomew became very excited. 'There's definitely something in there!'

Cautiously, I put my hand around to feel the site of the infection. Cringing, I felt something small and hard within the swollen tissue.

'Don't try and pull it out,' ordered my uncle. 'You need a precision instrument for this sort of work.'

He opened a drawer and pulled out a large pair of gleaming tweezers. I gritted my teeth against the pain as he dug them into my flesh and fished around. Finally the tweezers clamped onto something hard.

I swore out loud as he pulled whatever it was free, and more blood gushed down my back.

'What in the world is *that*?' I asked, revolted at the sight of the bloody lump he was holding up to the light.

I stared in horror. I couldn't believe my eyes!

7:18 pm

Bartholomew dropped the bloody lump into the sink and ran hot water over it until it shone clean.

'There's your carbuncle,' he said, placing it in the palm of my hand. We both stood staring at the object, no bigger than a tiny nail, with a circular drum-shaped head.

Even though I'd never seen one before, I knew what I was looking at.

'The bug,' I whispered. 'A tiny transmitter. When could they have done that?' I began, frantically racking my brain.

'No way!' I said, realising when it must have happened. 'When they abducted me in January! They knocked me unconscious and when I woke up my right shoulder was aching. It's been playing up ever since then!'

I looked at my great-uncle in disbelief. 'That's how they always know where I am. That's how they always track me down! That's how that rat Kelvin has been passing info on to Sligo! That's why Oriana's car's up there on Mount Helicon Road!'

Bartholomew straightened up. 'And that's what was interfering with my radio channel! It's been transmitting your whereabouts. It still is!'

He grabbed the shotgun. 'The low-down dirty crooks! They stuck it under your skin! An implant! Whoever they are, I'm going to deal with them,' said Bartholomew, fiercely loading the shotgun. 'And this time, I'm using live ammunition!'

'I've gotta get out of here,' I said. 'They'll be coming straight in at any second!'

Great-uncle Bartholomew grabbed my arm. 'No! *You've* got to stay here. But we'll make it *look* like you've left!'

The old man's face was glowing with excitement. He must have been crazy, I thought. I tried to reason with him. 'Great-uncle Bartholomew,' I said, 'if those people come in here and get me, it won't be just me they get. Don't you see? You're in danger too! We've gotta get out of here. But first, I'm going to destroy this thing!'

Great-uncle Bartholomew grabbed my arm, stopping me.

'I have a much better idea,' he said.

7:26 pm

He leaned the shotgun against the wall, seized the small transmitter from my hand and then went downstairs to the fridge and pulled out some beef mince.

'Please,' I tried again, thinking the guy was really going nuts, 'I've gotta get out of here. Don't you get it? You're in danger too!'

Bartholomew didn't answer me; instead, he looked up to the dark corner of the ceiling where Maggers perched on a small bracket. He whistled. Then he pressed the small electronic device into a juicy ball of meat and whistled again. This time I heard wings flapping. Maggers plopped down onto the table, steadying himself with his wings, then folded them and cocked his head at the food. He started eating greedily. Most of it went down quickly, including the bug. I looked at my great-uncle with new respect. The old guy was brilliant!

'Maggers doesn't like being disturbed at night,' said my great-uncle, 'but he'll have to put up with it. He's going on an important mission!'

I wondered how the magpie would cope with a small transmitter in his gut but my great-uncle must have read my mind.

'Don't worry about Maggers,' he said. 'I'm talking about the process of avian alimentary elimination. What is commonly called bird droppings. Nature will take its course. Have you seen the size of mistletoe seeds? Old Maggers won't even notice.'

Great-uncle Bartholomew picked the bird up and, stroking his head gently, took him upstairs. At the window at the end of the hallway, he gently threw Maggers into the night air. There were some squawks of protest and a flurry of black and white feathers, before Maggers spread his wings and flew towards the dense forest way beyond the clear paddocks that surrounded the house.

'What a pilot!' said Great-uncle Bartholomew, watching him with admiration. 'Night flying through trees without instruments. That should keep them entertained,' he chuckled.

I stared out the window but Maggers had already disappeared, swallowed up in the darkness. We took turns looking through the telescope. I watched with relief as the dark blue Mercedes that had parked on the roadside suddenly came to life, switched on its headlights and took off down the road towards the forested area, following the direction that Maggers had taken.

They'd fallen for it! Maggers had bought me more time.

7:37 pm

We went downstairs again and, not knowing how long Maggers would keep them away from us, we fortified the house as best we could. We pushed tables, heavy chairs and cupboards against the doors and locked all the windows. I knew it was only a matter of time before Oriana de la Force and her enforcers would be breathing down my neck again, but for the moment the heat was off.

Great-uncle Bartholomew put some sticking plaster on my right shoulder and put the kettle on. The night was very still. I liked thinking about Oriana's goons crashing around in the bush trying to find me. I hoped Maggers would take them a long way away.

Great-uncle Bartholomew grabbed his chest suddenly.

'You OK?' I asked, concerned.

'Ah, it's nothing. Not to worry.'

'How long do you think before they work out what's happened to the bug?' I asked.

'Could be days,' he chuckled. 'Let's hope.'

I wasn't so sure.

8:31 pm

'Uncle,' I said, as I dug around in my backpack, 'I think Dad had the Ormond Jewel. I reckon it was in his suitcase—the one that was sent to us by his landlady in Ireland. When we went through his clothes in it, we found this,' I held up the transparency with the two names on it, 'and an empty jewellery box. It was the first time Mum and I had ever seen it, but we didn't even know it was there until we were tidying up after the break-in at our house.'

'So you think the criminal gang that broke into your house pinched it?'

I nodded. '*Someone* took it. Do you know anything about it? I mean, what it looks like?'

Bartholomew took our empty soup bowls to the sink. 'Cal, I don't want to dampen your enthusiasm, but the chances of the Ormond Jewel surviving up to now are very slight.'

Suddenly a thought hit me like a bolt of lightning. 'That's where all the money went!'

'What money?'

With all the wild and crazy events of the last five months I'd almost forgotten how angry and hurt Mum had been by the news that Dad had taken almost every cent of their life savings.

'Dad withdrew over one hundred thousand dollars while he was in Ireland. We thought he'd lost his mind—that it was part of his illness. But what if he found the Ormond Jewel and bought it from someone?'

I could see my uncle looking at me in a very serious way. 'I suppose there's a chance that he tracked it down somewhere. You'd have to go to Ireland and find out where he bought it to be sure. But *I* can help you with something—I think there's a description of it somewhere in one of my books.'

Was this the prize that Vulkan Sligo and Oriana de la Force were after? Something didn't quite add up.

'The book is somewhere here,' said the old man, digging through endless piles of books and journals. 'It might take me a while to find it.'

8:55 pm

'Boges!' I shouted, as soon as he answered my

call. 'It's me!' I'd turned my phone on to ring him while Great-uncle Bartholomew was busy.

'Cal, how's it going, man? You made it to "Kilkenny"!'

'Yep, I'm cool, except for being bugged, but that's not why I'm ringing. Guess what? My great-uncle's told me all he knows about something called the Ormond *Jewel*. The Ormond Jewel!' I repeated. 'I reckon my dad had it!'

'The empty jewellery box!' Boges said excitedly. 'Do you think that's what the January break-in was all about?'

'I'm sure of it. Someone must have found out he had it, and then they stole it.'

'Of course. It could have been the massive prize your dad was holding onto!'

'That's what I thought at first,' I said, 'but remember, there was that *second* break-in when Gabbi got hurt—and I had to run for it. And that's the question,' I said, thinking fast, 'if the Ormond Jewel was the prize they were after, then why are *both* gangs still coming after me?'

Boges grunted on the other end of the line. 'Good point, dude.'

'It doesn't make sense. Sligo or Oriana might think I have the Jewel, but not both of them, because one of them has it already.'

'You're spot on. So tell me what you know about it.'

'My uncle has a description of it somewhere in a book here. He's looking for it right now. Plus he has some information on the Piers Ormond will. His house is kind of a mess, so finding what he's looking for could take some time. I'll call you back when I know more.'

'You said something about being bugged.'

'It's a bit of a long story, and it kinda begins and ends with a magpie.'

'Dude, you are sounding totally weird. Should I be worried?'

'Nah, mate, I'm cool. How about you—'

'Here it is!' I heard my great-uncle yell from where he was kneeling on the floor.

'Gotta go, Boges. I'll call you again soon.'

9:12 pm

Great-uncle Bartholomew stood up, brushed himself down, and carefully carried the old book over to the wing table. The ancient-looking book was bound in scruffy, tan leather, with faded gold lettering down the spine. The pages were stiff and yellowed with age. My great-uncle gently prised them apart until he came to the page he wanted.

'This is a contemporary description of the Ormond Jewel,' he said, 'written by a courtier.'

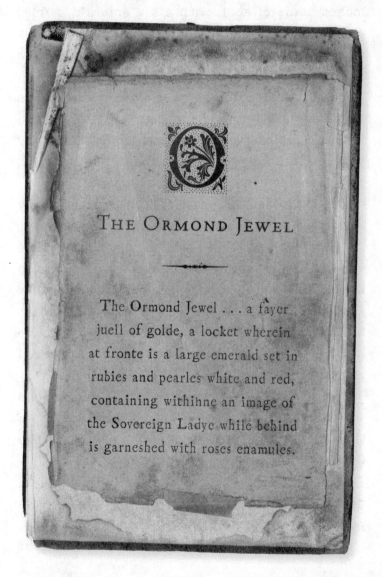

THE ORMOND JEWEL

The Ormond Jewel ... a fayer juell of golde, a locket wherein at fronte is a large emerald set in rubies and pearles white and red, containing withinne an image of the Sovereign Ladye while behind is garneshed with roses enamules.

'I think I get the picture,' I said, 'even with all that weird spelling. It sounds pretty cool—a locket made of gold, with a big emerald, rubies and pearls on the outside, and inside a picture of some great lady . . . and on the back, some enamelled roses.'

'Not just *any* lady,' interrupted Great-uncle Bartholomew, 'but *the* Sovereign Lady. The Queen herself. Probably a miniature. They were very popular in Tudor times. Instead of photographs, you gave someone a portrait of yourself.'

'So this Ormond Jewel,' I said, 'was given by the Queen to the Ormond family?'

'That's the story,' nodded my uncle. 'The virgin Queen—she never married—gave jewels to her favourites or to anyone who had done her good service. You should have a talk to my sister, Millicent. She's the historian of the family. She has all the family papers and documents. Me, I was always more interested in aeroplanes.'

'Millicent?' I was very keen to talk to anyone who might shed more light on the secret of the Ormonds. 'She might know more about the Ormond Singularity?' I asked.

But my great-uncle didn't answer me. Instead, he sat upright, a look of surprise on his face. He pointed to the drawings. 'Will you look at that!'

I peered over to see that he was jabbing at

the drawing of the waiter with the tray and winning combination of cards.

'That butler, with the tray,' he said. 'He's scored a blackjack!'

'That's right,' I said. 'That's what we've worked out, too. Except we didn't call him a butler, we thought he was a waiter,' I said, remembering then that Winter *had* actually referred to him as a *butler*.

My uncle's eyes softened as he looked at me. 'Tom's brain may have been scrambled, but he was trying to tell you something very important here,' he said, tapping the drawing. 'See what he's done? Maybe you didn't know that the family name Ormond comes from one of the great families of Ireland, the Butlers. The Butlers were the Earls and then later the Dukes of Ormond. You're descended from them a long way back.'

I stared at the butler and his tray with the cards. Another of the clues was falling into place!

'And I wonder,' said my great-uncle, 'if by drawing that pair of cards, the winning black-jack, your father was trying to tell you something about a particular one of the great Earls of Ormond in Ireland.'

There was a moment's silence until Great-uncle Bartholomew spoke again. 'What would you say,' he asked, 'if I told you that the tenth Earl's nickname was *Black Tom*? As in, Black Tom Butler, the tenth Earl of Ormond?'

I blinked. The drawing that I'd looked at hundreds of times, and puzzled over as many times, suddenly took on a new meaning. *Black* Jack. *Black* Tom *Butler.* Is that what Dad meant?

'It's strange how things that happened hundreds of years ago seem to have something to do with what Dad stumbled across in Ireland only last year,' I commented.

'Some things don't date,' said my uncle. 'Some things are always there, ticking away, just waiting to be discovered. They're still digging things out of the past. The passing of time doesn't change that.'

Is that what the Ormond Singularity was? Something that happened four hundred years ago still waiting to be discovered? I turned my attention back to my uncle.

'That reminds me,' he said. 'The family story is that the Ormond Jewel was given to Black Tom by his cousin, the Queen.'

'Black Tom was a cousin of the Queen?' I asked. 'The Sovereign Lady?'

'Uh-huh,' he nodded, 'and the Ormond Riddle was also associated with Black Tom.'

I carefully took in this new information—connecting the Ormond Riddle and the Ormond Jewel with some guy who'd been around four hundred years ago called Black Tom Butler. I liked the sound of this guy, with his pirate's name.

'Because if your father had the Ormond Jewel and knew about the Ormond Riddle, he was well on the way to—who knows what? There's always been this vague story in the family about the Riddle and the Jewel, that they have to be put together. Like a horse and cart. That both are needed . . . For what? I don't know. That's the great mystery.' He shrugged. 'Could be that they're both necessary for cracking the mystery of the Ormond Singularity—whatever that might be.'

My great-uncle shook his head. 'But I do know this much,' he continued, 'even if you solve the Ormond Riddle—and that's going to be hard enough without the last two lines—it's useless without the Ormond Jewel.'

My mind made a leap as I recalled Winter and the overheard conversation she mentioned. She'd picked up something about a double-key code!

'You have to have both,' I said slowly, 'because they are two halves of a double-key code. The Ormond Riddle is only half of the key. The

Ormond Jewel is the other half! Maybe the two combined reveal the Ormond Singularity!'

'I think you're onto something, Cal,' my uncle said, nodding.

'You say Black Tom was the tenth Earl. That means there were another nine before him, and maybe more after him. What's so special about him?'

'He was a great builder of castles and fortresses,' he said, and immediately I thought of Jennifer Smith and my dad's memory card, containing pictures of castles and ruins. 'He left a mark. A couple of his castles are still standing today and are open to the public. But most importantly, he's the earl connected with the Jewel and the Riddle. My sister Millicent told me when I was a boy that it's thought that Black Tom might have even written the Riddle. It was a time of great intrigue and secret codes were very necessary, especially if you had plans you didn't want anyone to know about. In those days, being on the wrong team meant you could lose your head for treason.'

'So the Ormond Riddle might be hiding a big secret?' I suggested.

'It's possible,' said my uncle.

I jumped as a piece of timber exploded in the fire. All this historical stuff was very complicated. But one thing was clear. If I wanted to find out Dad's secret, having the Ormond Riddle, even *with* the last two lines, wasn't enough. I had to find this Ormond Jewel. So just who had it now?

11:55 pm

I lay on my air mattress, awake for a long time, listening to the crackling of the dying fire, and hoping I wouldn't hear Oriana's car returning.

31 MAY

215 days to go . . .

4:50 pm

There'd been no sign of Maggers or that dark blue Mercedes all day and I wondered where the territorial magpie had taken my predators. Great-uncle Bartholomew was back amongst his books and papers, searching for the Piers Ormond documents that he had 'somewhere' in his massive mess.

'What do they look like?' I asked, trying to help. 'What exactly am I looking for?'

My uncle stood up from where he'd been crouching. 'I put them in a big envelope and tucked them in a book, I remember. It was a large envelope with a solicitor's address on it somewhere. But I don't remember which book.' He looked around, sheepishly. 'Maybe it wasn't even a book. Could have been a magazine.'

I looked around in despair. The place was full of aviation magazines. Somewhere in all these piles of books and magazines there might be an envelope. There was only one thing to do—we'd have to go through every single one.

6:34 pm

We'd almost finished checking through every journal and book on the ground floor. I had one last box to go through—old flying magazines. I tried not to be too distracted by the photographs and stories. It reminded me of when I was a little kid and how I used to go through Dad's flying magazines, cutting out the aeroplanes I liked and sticking them in my scrapbook, hoping one day I could fly my own.

I had almost come to the bottom of the box when I saw a piece of yellowing newspaper sticking out from a magazine. The headline caught my attention:

TWIN BABY ABDUCTION NIGHTMARE

I moved closer to the nearby lamp and started to read it when I was aware of a presence behind me. Spooked, I turned to find Great-uncle Bartholomew leaning over me. Very quickly he whisked the old piece of newsprint out of my hand.

'Stop wasting time reading that old stuff!' he ordered. 'I thought you needed to find the Piers Ormond documents!'

I was startled at the look of pain and anger on his face.

'I didn't mean to pry. I was just—'

'Never mind what you were just doing! We've finished the search down here. It's time to go upstairs and start there. Hurry up!'

I got to my feet, shocked at how my great-uncle had snapped at me. What was so wrong with looking at a bit of old newspaper? It was just another sad story. He'd acted as though I was doing something bad. Puzzled, I went upstairs and tried to forget about it.

9:03 pm

I'd just made it through another carton, upstairs, when a familiar sound caught my attention. I looked down the hallway to see Maggers fluttering at the upstairs window. My great-uncle saw him too and went running down the hall and opened it.

'No! No, Maggers!' he shouted. 'Go away! Go flying! Quick, hurry up!'

But Maggers did no such thing. Instead of flying up and into the night sky, he flipped through the window and into the house, soaring along the hallway and then flying downstairs to land on the wing table where he waited for us expectantly.

We raced downstairs after him. Again, Great-uncle Bartholomew tried to coax him outside. But it was no use, he wouldn't budge.

'He's hungry,' said Bartholomew, reaching for the mince in the fridge. 'He's probably forgotten how to feed himself. I'll give him something to eat and send him on his way again. Otherwise your *friends* will be down on us like a ton of bricks!'

Great-uncle Bartholomew suddenly stopped his actions, put his knife down and looked at me, his eyes wide. 'Glory be! I've just remembered! I put those documents in the wedding photo album! My ex has it! She took the albums, I'm sure of it!'

I took a deep, frustrated breath. 'So where is she now?'

'Not far away enough,' he muttered.

Maggers had pecked up almost all the meat by now and I was anxious that he should be out and about—flying a long way away from here.

'Tell me where she lives now and I'll go there straight away,' I said.

'You know what I said about the neighbour who uses his shotgun for real?'

I nodded.

'She lives with him. Across those paddocks over there,' Great-uncle Bartholomew pointed out the kitchen window. I came up behind him to see where he meant. 'Beyond those trees that you can see just to the right, near that dip in the hill, is his house. The one with the orangey glow, and tall windmill turning by the water tank. It doesn't look like his truck's there.'

'I could be there in ten minutes,' I said, 'look through the album, get the documents and be back again in under half an hour.'

But my great-uncle was staring sightlessly out of the kitchen window, as if he hadn't heard me at all. 'She was a handful, my ex-wife. After she ran away with our next-door neighbour, I found she'd taken all sorts of things, including the albums. People round here think I'm a cranky old fool because I discourage visitors. But I've never shot anyone. My shotgun's purely for show. But that's not the case with Barney Helstrom. When he pulls out the shotgun, he is dead serious. Perfect mate for my ex-wife. But that's another story.' My great-uncle's face had turned quite red. 'Plus he's got two rottweiler-dingo-cross dogs,' he continued. 'The meanest set of eight legs you could imagine. He calls them "Skull" and "Crossbones". They're hounds from your worst nightmare!'

'I'm going to try to get inside and find the album,' I said. 'I have to get my hands on those papers about Piers Ormond.'

'It's very dangerous,' said my great-uncle. 'Not just because of the dogs . . . if Barney finds you in his house . . .'

'I'm writing my mobile number down,' I said as I scribbled it on a piece of paper. 'If you see him coming, give me a ring to warn me and I'll get out as fast as I can.' My voice sounded brave and bold but inside I was quivering.

'But the dogs . . .' my great-uncle began.

'Oriana's thugs are really dangerous,' I said, cutting his words short. 'Make sure you have plenty of ammo, just in case they show up.'

'Don't worry about me, Cal. I could hold them off for days. It's you I'm concerned about. I don't want anything happening to you.'

A sound from outside silenced him and I strained to hear what it was, hoping that it wasn't what I thought it was.

It was the sound of a car.

They had followed Maggers!

I ran to the front door and peered through, the leadlight glass distorting the view. Despite that, the dark blue Mercedes was plain to see, its headlights shining down from the road.

9:51 pm

I didn't need any urging. I bolted out the back kitchen door, jumped the triple-wire fence separating my great-uncle's rundown garden from the paddocks beyond, and ran through the long grass, my backpack bumping along on my still tender shoulder.

As I ran across the clear paddocks, I kept low, trying not to make too much of a moving silhouette, using any cover that was available—bushes and small trees along the fence margins as far as I could. I hoped Great-uncle Bartholomew would be OK, barricaded into his house with his shottie and his piles of ammo. Even if they did get into his place, there'd be no trace of me.

I thought fleetingly of my great-uncle's weird reaction to the newspaper clipping I'd found about the abduction of two babies, but I had other things to worry about right now, because I had almost reached the trees that my great-uncle had pointed out to me through the window.

The hairs on the back of my neck stood up.

Already I could hear the sound of dogs howling and barking. They'd picked up my scent! I froze. Anyone in the house would be alerted by now that there was a visitor on the way. For a moment I didn't know what to do. I could hear the savagery in their howls, the viciousness in their barking.

The barking became more frenzied as I approached the small, timber, two-storeyed house. I was relieved to see a tall wire fence that ran around the perimeter. Two large dogs, one yellow like the dingoes he partly came from, the other wearing the brownish-black of the rottweilers, were hurling themselves against the netting. Even at a distance and in the dark, I could see their piercing white teeth.

But no-one came outside to see what the ruckus was all about. Great-uncle Bartholomew's ex-wife and Helstrom must not be at home.

I had to find a way past the dogs. I glanced over at my great-uncle's place, now just a distant shape beyond the paddocks. I wondered what was happening there, but the barking quickly drew my attention back to where I was crouched.

'Slow down, and observe,' my dad used to say to me when we were out fishing in the tinny. 'After a while, you'll start to see where the fish are. You'll see how the water is moving, where the warm eddies are, and you'll start to see the tiny fish that attract the bigger fish. If you're still, things will often reveal themselves.' I used to think, 'Yeah, yeah, yeah, OK Dad.' But now his words started to really mean something.

I soon saw that the way into the house lay in the surrounding trees. Since I'd been on the run, I'd had to use trees a couple of times to get out of trouble or as observation posts. A big oak tree, its leaves already brown and dying, was growing near enough to the fence for me to get a hold of it. Then, like Tarzan, I hoped to move from tree to tree, keeping out of the reach of the two dogs.

I stood up, took a deep breath and made a huge running jump at the wire fence.

The two insane, mongrel dogs launched at me and snapped at my toes and hands as I pulled myself up to the top of the fence. I grabbed the nearest bough of the oak tree, and let go of the top of the wire fence. For a moment I thought it was going to break and that the dogs were going to eat me alive after I crashed to the ground, but the bough held. Arm over arm, like some sort of human gibbon, I worked my way along. With great relief I reached the trunk of the tree, scrambling onto a central fork.

It wasn't high enough! One of the leaping

hounds jumped up and grabbed my sneaker, clamping down on it hard, trying to shake me out of the tree. I couldn't believe its strength and ferocity. I wrapped my arms around the oak tree's solid trunk, clinging on, while the two dogs did everything they could to dislodge me. I could feel teeth as they dug deeper into my foot, trying to get a better grip.

Fearfully, I looked down at the yellow dog and just as it lurched to get my foot deeper into its mouth, I kicked as hard as I could. The dog let go for an instant and that gave me my chance. I practically flew up into the tree, reaching out and grabbing the branches of a smaller tree which was intermingled with the oak. I hauled myself across while the two dogs, enraged at my escape, tried even harder to jump up to get me. They clawed deep scrape marks into the trunks, and slobbered wildly, sending trails of frothy spittle over the dusty ground.

I couldn't waste any more time watching them. Now I had to jump and grab the railings of the small verandah on the second floor. Without thinking too much about it, I launched myself with all my strength into the air.

10:06 pm

I made it! I grabbed the timber rails and swung

my feet into the guttering that ran along in front of the verandah, then I pulled myself over the railings, safe from the dogs. I hoped that Barney Helstrom and his partner would stay away long enough for the next part of my search.

Two double doors that opened onto the verandah were locked but when I pushed on them they moved a little. With the dogs snapping and howling beneath me, and gun-happy Barney Helstrom possibly showing up at any time, I didn't care too much about his property. I kicked at the doors. On the third kick, they flew open and I fell inside.

I was in a bedroom. A quick check of the drawers and cupboards revealed nothing I needed. I hurried into the next room, which was an office, but all I could find were old accounts, farming books and novels. I was starting to get anxious.

I rushed downstairs to a central living area where, on a coffee table near a window, I saw a pile of albums. I went through them. The first one was full of old photographs taken at 'Kilkenny', showing my great-uncle's ex-wife, a nice-looking, dark-haired woman I'd never met before, with Great-uncle Bartholomew. I was shocked to see that in every photo my great-uncle's face had been aggressively scratched out or blackened.

I picked up the second one as my mobile rang, making me jump. I snatched it up.

'Barney Helstrom's car is on its way down the road,' my great-uncle puffed. 'You've got about one minute before they pull up outside the house.' His voice was strained and hoarse; his breathing raspy in his throat.

'What is it?' I asked. 'What's wrong?'

'Don't worry. It's my heart. All this excitement.' There was a sudden crash as he dropped the phone. I heard a groaning noise at the other end of the line.

'Uncle Bart!' I yelled down the line. 'Talk to me!'

All I could hear was silence. I shoved my mobile back into my pocket and grabbed the next album, shaking it, turning it upside down, flipping through its pages. I had to get out of there. Something was wrong with my great-uncle and Barney Helstrom was only a minute away. I tipped the third album up when a heavy envelope, just as my uncle had described, slid out onto the floor. I snatched it, jammed it into the back of my jeans, and hightailed it up the stairs again, through the bedroom and straight out of the wide-open double doors.

The dogs downstairs went wild once more! I jumped up onto the top of the railing on the small verandah and launched again into the tree. When all this was over, I thought, I'd be able to get a job in a circus. If I lived long enough.

Beneath me, the dogs were revving up, frothing at the mouth, ears flattened back on their heads. I was really pumped—worried about my great-uncle and worried for myself. I had no idea how I was going to get out of this. My heart was racing, my hands were sweating as I grabbed at handfuls of leaves, not caring about the scratches and scrapes to my face and hands as I pushed on through the tree, thinking only of keeping myself high enough to avoid the jaws of the dogs.

And now I had another problem! I could hear a car in the distance. Barney Helstrom was on his way home and that meant trouble—big time! I hurled myself around to the other side of the tree and leaned right over, trying to grab the branches of the oak tree, my original point of entry. The sound of the returning car had driven the dogs into another frenzy.

I was leaning forward, trying again to reach the branches, when the yellow dog jumped up, thrusting its snout almost into my face. I lost my balance and twisted, falling heavily.

I rolled over, getting back on my feet as fast as I could—I didn't want to be on the ground with two savage dogs in my face. I took off in a sprint, making a dash for the windmill.

I flew towards the windmill, taking a running jump at the lowest part of the scaffolding. But as I did so, both dogs did the same, their jaws wide open and ready to clamp down on me. Before I knew it, I was hanging from the windmill with a dog attached to each of my legs.

I heard a ripping sound, as one leg of my jeans tore right off below the knee, sending the yellow dog head over heels backwards. The other dog seemed to tug twice as hard in the absence of his friend, and within seconds both of them were on me again.

I was struggling to keep my grip. I could hear the car idling near the gates, followed by the gates being dragged open. The weight of the dogs was wrenching me down and although I tried to hang on with every ounce of strength left in my fingers, every second my energy was draining away.

It wouldn't be long before I was dragged back off the windmill and Helstrom would pick up whatever scraps the dogs left of me.

My fingers were numbing, loosening, the strength ebbing away from them, when a miracle occurred. Both dogs let go!

I dropped down to the grass and scrambled

up over the boundary fence. A quick glance back as I got to my feet revealed what had happened. As soon as their owners had come through the gates and stepped out of the car, the dogs had lost all interest in me and bounded over to greet them.

I put my head down and kept running.

10:23 pm

I was almost back at Great-uncle Bartholomew's property when a shot rang out. I dived to the ground. Barney Helstrom had taken a shot at me! I leopard-crawled the rest of the way, my heart racing, my legs weak from running and terror.

I squeezed through the triple-wire fence and was about to stand up and run when I saw something that made my blood run cold. Facing away from me, the dark blue Mercedes was parked along the side of Great-uncle Bartholomew's house! I could see the occupants of the car deep in discussion. Sumo Wrestler had his arm in a sling—he was probably still healing from his gunshot wound from last month—and he seemed to be arguing with Kelvin, the teardrop tattoo guy, who was sitting in the driver's seat.

Hardly daring to look at them, and keeping as low as I could, I crept to the back kitchen door, cautiously opening and closing it again fast. Once inside, I locked it, and dragged the heavy kitchen table over against it. Although my first impulse was to check on my great-uncle, I wanted to make the house as safe as possible again—for both our sakes. When I felt I had the back door reasonably secured, I charged my way through the boxes, parts and piles of aviation magazines until I was at the front door. I checked the three locks were bolted, then gave the ancient hallstand we'd earlier shoved behind it, another push, manoeuvring it further into position by brute force.

By this stage I was panting with exhaustion. I slid down the wall and sat on the floor for a moment, getting my breath. I looked at my scraped fingers, bloody and deeply indented with red furrows from where the scaffolding of the windmill had dug into my skin. I jumped back up and hurried upstairs, calling out to my great-uncle.

10:34 pm

He didn't answer. I paused on the landing, aware of the great stillness in the house that just didn't feel right.

'Uncle Bart?' I shouted again.

I kicked open each of the upstairs rooms.

Something was wrong, seriously wrong, I knew it.

When I saw him lying still on the floor near the telescope, I feared the worst. I raced over to him, dropping to my knees beside his outflung body.

'Bartholomew! What's happened? Are you OK?!'

He was breathing. I carefully lifted his head and shoulders up, propping him on a couple of old leather flying jackets. He opened his eyes.

'My heart . . . Did you . . . find the documents from the solicitor?' he asked me, softly and slowly.

'I did.'

'Read,' he said between gasps for breath, 'me the letter.'

'No, Uncle, you need help. I'm just going to grab my phone and call for help.'

I was scared. For the first time this year, I'd found a relative who was not only completely on my side, but eager to help me. And now he was almost lifeless on the floor. All thought of my own danger had left me. I had to help him.

'I'm just going to call an ambulance, OK.'

'It's too late,' said the old man. 'Too late for that, Cal.'

'Don't say that,' I said, tears rising, as my

great-uncle struggled to lift his head. His face was a deathly shade of white.

'What's that . . . noise downstairs?' he asked, his voice nothing but a raspy whisper. 'Where's my shotgun?'

'Don't be crazy. Just stay there and rest,' I said, thinking I'd run and get the gun myself.

But it *was* too late for that—I could now hear the noise downstairs, too, as Oriana de la Force's henchmen tried to bash their way into the house. 'It's those people who are after me,' I said, looking into his worried eyes. 'They're here. They're trying to get in!'

'Open the envelope,' said my uncle, from the floor. 'Read it to me.'

'But, you—'

'Do as I tell you!'

I ripped open the envelope, pulling out the letter from inside. It was from Tweedie, Makepeace and Associates, a legal firm with an address in the city. I skim-read it—trying to make sense of it. I read enough to discover that the Piers Ormond will was no longer in their possession. It had been transferred to the Ormond family solicitor as per the receipt. Included was a photocopy of the signed receipt, presumably done by whoever had picked up the Ormond will, but it was illegible.

Downstairs, the bashing on the front door was getting louder and I could hear the sounds of timber splintering and glass smashing. A few more minutes and Kelvin and Sumo would be inside! The old man and I would be no match for the two of them.

My great-uncle started coughing—a terrible, grating sound from deep in his throat. I dropped the letter and tried to make him more comfortable, propping him higher so that he could breathe more easily.

A strange smell wafted up the hall. I sniffed the air. Smoke!

Had they set fire to the house?!

I ran to the landing. Thin streams of smoke climbed into the air. I couldn't see fire anywhere, but the smoke was getting thicker as I watched. Were they trying to smoke me out of the house?

A black column of smoke suddenly clouded up the staircase, and I realised I *could* hear the crackle of fire, coming from somewhere downstairs.

'Great-uncle Bartholomew,' I said, crouching by his side again. 'We've gotta get you out of here! Now! The house is on fire!'

But the old man had closed his eyes, his breathing now coming in shorter, more infrequent gasps. He looked frail and so much older, his clothes draping off his body onto the floor. The skin of his face seemed stretched, like pale parchment.

He made a huge effort and opened his eyes again, struggling to speak. 'Did you get the name,' he whispered, 'the name of the solicitor who has the Piers Ormond will?'

'There's no time for that,' I urged. 'We've gotta get out of here. The place is on fire! We've gotta get you out and to the hospital!'

I ran over to the top of the stairs and looked down.

I was horrified at what I saw. The hallway was already ablaze, and the fire was moving towards the large living room. Our only chance lay in getting quickly down the staircase before it, too, was eaten by flames.

10:56 pm

'They say your whole life passes before you while you are dying,' whispered my great-uncle as I ran back to him, frantically trying to work out the best way to move him. 'I don't have much time left. I can already hear the chief pilot calling.'

In the days that I'd spent with Great-uncle Bartholomew, we'd become very close. He *believed* my story; he wanted to help me. I refused to believe that I was about to lose him.

'Don't say that! You've got to let me help you get out of here,' I cried. 'Come *on*! I'll help you down the stairs. You'll be all right!'

I had to put my ear right down to his mouth to hear what he was saying.

'You've got to get out of here, Cal,' he said. 'But before you go, I . . . I want to tell you something. The kidnapping of those babies . . . that you read about. One of them . . . one of them . . . is you . . . you . . . you have to go now. Get out. Please. I don't have time to tell you everything . . . I think I've remembered the young solicitor's name . . . So hard. So hard to speak . . . A young fellow from Mount Helicon.' He gulped, slowly. 'But now . . . now you have to go. Leave me here.'

The fire roared closer to the staircase. Hot embers whirled past us in a devilish dance.

'I can't leave you here!' I protested.

'I'm already on my way out,' gasped my uncle. 'I only have a few more breaths left in me. I can't waste them . . . arguing with you. Take the Orca. Please. I think it will fly.'

'The Orca?' I asked, so afraid of what was coming.

'Only one stick,' he said, 'the thrust lever.'

The smoke thickened around us. It filled the

upstairs landing and I could feel the heat of the fire rising.

'Don't use the rockets . . . they're untested . . . could be too powerful. Fly to Dimityville Airfield. About seventy kilometres away. Almost due north.' He grabbed my hand. 'Now go . . . before it's too late.'

I dug my hands underneath his shoulders and started to lift him.

'Stop!' he moaned, before coughing and wheezing, trying to suck air in. 'Don't forget the solicitor's name,' he ordered. 'You *must* remember. This person has the Piers Ormond will.'

He began whispering the name again and again, insisting that I repeat it for him. I parroted the name, but I was hardly concentrating. I was already coughing, my throat and lungs were filling with toxic smoke.

I ran to the top of the staircase again to see the flames running along the floorboards below. The aircraft-wing table was ablaze and fire licked the curtains of the living room. Any moment now and the staircase would catch fire and the flames would leap into the second floor. The heat and smoke were already tremendous and growing hotter and darker with every passing moment. I ran back to my uncle.

'Bartholomew!' I cried, shovelling under his shoulders again, preparing to drag him. 'Let's go!'

'Stop!' he cried once more, grabbing my hand and squeezing it with all of his strength. I looked down to see that he'd placed the Orca canopy keys in my palm.

'Please,' he continued, 'it's too late . . . for me. I have to go now,' he whispered. 'Goodbye, Cal . . . Tom would be . . . so proud of his boy . . . Good luck on your journey.'

With that, he fell back.

11:05 pm

It took me a few seconds to realise that Great-uncle Bartholomew was dead. There was no heartbeat. No rise and fall of his chest. He was silent and still. It was like when Dad died and his face changed. I remember thinking as I looked at him that whoever had been living in my dad's familiar body was no longer there. I saw the same thing in my great-uncle's face. His features were exactly the same, but the real person—the eccentric aviator—had definitely flown away.

I tightened my grip on the keys he had given me, and wiped hot tears from my face.

'Good luck on your journey, too, Great-uncle Bartholomew,' I whispered.

I jumped to my feet, pulled on one of the old leather jackets, grabbed another one for cover, slung my backpack over my shoulder and ran to the top of the stairs.

The Ormond Orca had never flown, and now I was going to be the test pilot. What if Bartholomew hadn't got it right and it exploded the moment I pressed the starter?

Either way, I had to get out of the house. If I didn't leave now, there'd be no possibility of a flight!

The heat coming up from the fire was really scaring me now. 'Kilkenny' had become a death trap. I stumbled downstairs through the choking smoke, ducking out of the way of fiery embers, hopping over the tendrils of flame that were running along the floorboards, weaving my way around obstacles that I could hardly see any more.

The roar of the inferno was terrifying and the house seemed to shake with the intensity of the blaze. I dropped to my knees and crawled along on the floor, where I could breathe better, and felt my way to the kitchen, which had so far escaped the full force of the flames.

I paused to work out what I was going to do next. I had no idea where Sumo or Kelvin might be. If they were waiting for me out the back, I had to get past them.

The smoke was really getting to me now and I had to leave the house or I'd choke to death. I kicked the burning table out of my way and opened the back door. There was an explosion of flames behind me. I had created a draught of oxygen and the fire reared up, a bigger monster than before! I slammed the door behind me and made a beeline for the shed.

The sound of smashing glass and a bloodcurdling yell startled me. I turned back and saw Kelvin rolling on the ground, bleeding, and surrounded by broken glass. The front windows of the house had blown out in the extreme heat, cutting Kelvin down with flying shards of glass. I could hear curses from Sumo although I couldn't see where he was.

Kelvin staggered to his feet, blood gushing down his forehead. Through the red haze he spotted me. 'There he is! Don't let him get away!' he shouted.

Sumo came running after me as I was wrenching open the shed door. In the nick of time I slammed it behind me, locking it. I clutched the canopy keys in my hand, scrambled up onto the wing, opened the Ormond Orca, threw my backpack across onto the co-pilot's seat, and jumped into position.

I'd never flown anything like this machine, but it was my only chance. If I hesitated, I had no chance at all—Kelvin and Sumo would make it round to the other side of the shed and pounce, savagely ripping me out of the Orca and dragging me back to their boss.

I scanned the controls, taking in the details. Some I knew—the fuel gauge, the airspeed indicator, the artificial horizon . . . but all my experience as a pilot had been in a Cessna 172 and I'd always had Dad sitting beside me.

Beside the thrust lever that my great-uncle mentioned was a row of switches. One was for the battery, which I flicked on. Next to it was the power and the fuel, which I also flicked on. A switch marked RATO—Rocket Assisted Take-Off—reminded me of my uncle's warning against using it. I wouldn't touch that button.

I started the ignition and the turbine started whining. I could hear Sumo and Kelvin outside, bashing on the rear door of the shed. They hadn't realised that the front doors were open!

The jet was slow in warming up and as we lumbered out through the open doors ahead and started bouncing over the uneven paddock ground, I turned back to see Sumo and Kelvin running towards the Mercedes.

The little jet trundled down the rough airstrip. 'Get a move on!' I urged. I pulled on the thrust lever but it was still taking me way too long to get up enough speed for take-off.

The Mercedes was already coming for me, tearing dust up behind it, and quickly gaining ground. 'Hurry up, Orca,' I begged as we slowly picked up speed.

The wind whistled past my face; I'd completely forgotten to close the canopy! I couldn't waste time just now closing it—the Mercedes had gained on the aircraft and was almost alongside me!

Either of them could easily rip me out of the seat if they got up on the wing and clawed their way to me, and I could see that's exactly what they had in mind. They were enraged that I'd got away, and now their car raced along beside me on my right—Sumo was almost standing out of the passenger seat, his sausage-like arms shaking in my direction.

Something on my left flew into my peripheral vision. I took a second to glance over. It was Maggers, flying over me like a guardian angel. He suddenly dipped one wing, and then soared away.

I quickly turned back to the Mercedes, just in time to see Sumo swing out and catch hold of the right-hand wing.

He heaved himself up onto it, his weight causing the jet to tip and slow down.

I wasn't going fast enough for take-off. Somehow, I had to shake him off! Sumo reached closer, his evil grin almost on top of me!

There was only one thing to do, despite my great-uncle's warning!

Just as Sumo's huge hand reached for me, I leaned away and wrenched the canopy closed. He crawled around and started bashing on the front of the glass, looking like a giant bug on a windscreen. But I knew he wasn't going to be there for much longer.

I took a deep breath, jerked up the thrust lever and hit the RATO button.

The Orca suddenly lurched forward at tremendous speed and within seconds we'd launched off the ground! Sumo's face looked horrified as his body was ripped off the aircraft, and sent spinning to the ground.

I was shooting upwards, pinned to my seat!

I retracted the landing gear, taking note that the suggested speed for lowering them again when landing was around 150 kilometres per hour.

The Ormond Orca surged up and away, just like the adrenaline inside me, rockets blazing. The power and lift were unbelievable! I started praying it wouldn't explode, but the frame held firm.

We were airborne and climbing at a crazy thirty-degree angle! It was awesome! What an amazing aircraft!

'Goodbye Great-uncle Bartholomew,' I said under my breath. 'Safe journey and happy landing. I'll never forget you.'

11:39 pm

I glanced at the controls. Unbelievably, I was already passing five thousand feet! The Ormond Orca shot skywards like a homesick angel.

We continued to climb, the roar of the full-throttled engine filling my ears. I'd reached seven thousand feet without even trying, and now it was eight thousand, nine thousand—all in less than a minute.

The angle at which I could see the world beneath me eased as the RATO system cut out. I levelled out and stabilised, flying at 300 knots. Beneath me, nearly ten thousand feet below, 'Kilkenny' blazed.

11:41 pm

I'd escaped from Oriana's goons, once more, but at what cost? I felt tears sting my eyes as I thought of my great-uncle Bartholomew lying dead in his burning house. The fire had engulfed his entire existence, destroying his home, his work, his books, magazines and journals . . . his life. I'd just got to know the old guy and now he was gone. His heart just wasn't strong enough for what I'd brought to him. I felt sure he'd still be alive if those two thugs hadn't shown up at 'Kilkenny' and started terrorising us . . . or if I'd never shown up.

I thought about poor Maggers, left alone, and homeless. One day, I promised myself, I'd come back to 'Kilkenny', or what was left of it, and make sure Maggers was looked after.

I tried to put the sad thoughts out of my mind by concentrating on flying the Orca. Go to Dimityville Airfield, he'd told me. I didn't exactly have a flight plan, but almost due north ahead I could see the lights of a small township. As I jetted high above the earth, I fiddled with the dials on the radio, picking up the weather report. Luckily, even though I was flying through a night sky for the first time in my life, the conditions were clear. The moon was full—brilliant and bright like an aerial lighthouse.

11:45 pm

My mind ticked over the information I'd gathered with Great-uncle Bartholomew. The road to Dad's great secret had even more twists and turns in it than I first realised. My job now was to get this jet down safely, connect with Boges, and then start the search for the Ormond Jewel—which along with the Riddle formed the double-key code.

Sadness crept up on me again in the darkness. I found myself thinking about the last time I went flying, with Dad, well over a year ago. I also suddenly felt fear overcoming me. I'd never flown solo. I'd never flown at night. And I sure hadn't ever flown a jet before.

It's not so hard getting an aeroplane up in the air, but putting it down safely is a completely different matter. I'd landed the Cessna a couple of times but never on my own. Dad had always been beside me, ready to take over the controls if necessary. I didn't know what a jet would feel like—how it would handle on final approach . . . I'd never handled retractable landing gear, for a start. Basically, what I was flying *was an experimental aeroplane on its first test flight.*

The full reality of the situation I'd put myself in hit me, and at the same time a red light appeared on the control panel next to the fuel gauge. I couldn't believe my eyes! The fuel gauge was showing empty!

My panic rose rapidly. For some reason I was running out of fuel!

I've just got to put it down safely, I repeated, trying to calm myself down, just like my dad, or my great-uncle, would have done had they been sitting next to me.

I aimed for the township and began my descent. As I approached, I saw with relief that it was in fact Dimityville. I could read the huge letters spelling the name out, lit up on the roof of a warehouse.

The needle in the fuel gauge continued to show empty. According to the instruments, there was nothing in the tanks, but the Ormond Orca kept flying. Maybe I'd make it OK. Just maybe.

As the Orca sped closer and lower to the Dimityville airstrip, my heart nearly stopped. Beside the brilliantly lit runway, the red-and-blue flashing lights of police vehicles were there, waiting for me! A reception committee for when I landed—*if* I landed! Kelvin and Sumo must have dobbed me in!

I flew over some low cloud that I hoped would hide me from the welcoming committee on the ground. I needed to get on the other side of it, which looked to be only a short distance away. But as I flew around it, the cloud suddenly closed up, completely surrounding me. All I could see was white—beside, above and below me. It was what pilots call being inside the 'milk bottle'.

I felt like I couldn't breathe. Panic sucked the air out of my chest. I'd never had any real training on IFR—instrument flight rules. Without instrument rating, I had to rely on VFR—visual flight rules—for flying, and now I'd lost visual contact with my position. I was doomed! It was impossible to fly an aeroplane without reference to the horizon!

I was becoming disoriented, surrounded by dense cloud wherever I looked. I stared at the instrument panel. The artificial horizon had tilted, yet I felt that I was flying straight and level. I tried to correct my altitude, but my instincts were telling me the altitude indicator was *wrong*. Surely I could tell just by feeling in my body whether I was left or right, straight or tilted. Dad had told me about a test with experienced pilots flying in white-out without instruments in the simulator. Every single one of them went into the dreaded graveyard spin which meant three simple words; crash, burn, die.

Sweat broke out all over me. Again I could hear Dad's voice, 'If in cloud, don't trust your instincts, trust your instruments; they may be faulty but they are your best hope.'

I corrected the pitch of the aeroplane according to what the artificial horizon was telling me. A surge of relief flowed through me as I saw a break in the cloud.

I flew out. The altimeter told me I was a thousand feet above Dimityville Airfield, which was crawling with cops!

I made a fast decision. In the distance, beyond the Dimityville airstrip, I could see a floodlit football oval, beyond a forested area and a large dam. I had to throw the cops off my trail, at least for enough time to make a getaway.

First, I had to find a way of surviving a forced landing!

I pulled the throttle back to slow the Ormond Orca and flew a circuit of the airfield. I lowered the nose. Now we were doing about 150 kilometres per hour. One hundred and fifty! That was the suggested speed to engage the landing gear! I quickly engaged, and the heavy clunk of the gear readying itself under the aeroplane slowed us even more. I turned towards the Dimityville landing strip. I experimented with the flaps, taking them down a couple of notches.

So far, so good.

The cops were no doubt rubbing their hands with glee, expecting me to land on the strip below in a minute or so. I just prayed this fuel from nowhere would keep on going. I couldn't turn into a glider now: I needed lots of forward thrust for what I had in mind.

At five hundred feet the Ormond Orca was descending at around 85 knots and I was almost at the flare, preparing the jet for landing, when I suddenly slammed the throttle up and the little jet screamed back up into the sky and turned over the heads of the waiting cops.

I whooped and yelled as I climbed to two thousand feet and headed towards my real landing destination.

Behind me, I saw them all scrambling, getting back into their cars.

The clouds were lower now and I flew through a break. My escape was covered by thick blankets of creamy, moonlit billows.

I pushed the stick down, losing altitude. The roar of the jet changed into a whine, a falling tone that could only mean one thing. The miracle fuel had stopped flowing. Whatever had been left in the fuel lines was gone.

I pulled up the stick fast. I had to focus on surviving this landing! If I didn't, everything stopped with me.

I had to fly the jet without power. The icy fear fuelled by adrenaline cleared my head and gave me a cold determination. *I would land the Orca!*

I couldn't lose everything now. I'd come too far, suffered too much. I couldn't waste the hard work of my best friend Boges. Or even Winter Frey. I needed to be around for Gabbi . . . and my mum. And I especially couldn't let my dad, or Bartholomew, down.

11:52 pm

Thick forest lay ahead and beneath me. I lowered the nose and aimed for the flat area that I could just make out at the end of the football oval. I held the Ormond Orca at 150 knots and put the flaps right down.

I was coming in low now, across the tree tops at two hundred then one hundred feet. I was approaching a wire fence. Everything was rocketing past in a blur. I was still coming in way too fast!

It was almost time for impact. My body tensed. I held my breath.

I made it across the fence but then the Orca slammed into the ground hard. We bounced once, then twice, and on the third bounce, the nose wheel dug into the earth, ploughing it up and tearing it off. The Orca skidded sideways, driving me hard against the harness.

We were heading for the dam!

Another bounce and this time, with a massive

crash, the Ormond Orca cartwheeled and hit the dirt at a crazy angle.

The harness held me tight in my seat but my head had been thrown around violently. I yelled out in shock.

Time seemed to stand still. Everything started to go fuzzy.

I felt myself drifting out of consciousness, when I realised smoke was filling the cabin. Desperately I tried to undo my harness, but the buckle had been crushed and wouldn't open.

Crash, burn, die. Crash, burn, die, kept running through my mind like an evil spell.

I had to get out. The smoke was already blinding me, making me cough, ravaging my throat that was already scorched from the fire at 'Kilkenny'.

If this aeroplane exploded, I was done for!

I had to get out. If the explosion didn't kill me, smoke inhalation would. I gasped for air.

My fingers scrabbled around the floor—I remembered seeing Great-uncle Bartholomew's pocket knife somewhere when I first climbed in.

When I finally found the cold, metal tool, I picked it up and flicked out the blade. I sawed through the mesh of the harness until I was free.

Now I had to find the lever that opened the canopy!

I could hardly see anything, and I couldn't find it with my desperate fingers!

I was trapped. The smoke and heat were becoming unbearable!

IS RACE AGAINST TIME 06:48 07:12 05:21 RACE AG
CE AGAINST TIME SEEK THE TRUTH ... CONSPIRAC
E SOMETHING IS SERIOUSLY MESSED UP HERE 08
06 06:07 MAY WHO CAN CAL TRUST? SEEK THE T
04 10:08 RACE AGAINST TIME 02:27 08:06 10:32
E TRUTH 01:00 07:57 SOMETHING IS SERIOUSLY
01 09:53 CONSPIRACY 365 12:00 RACE AGAINST T
Y WHO CAN CAL TRUST? 01:09 LET THE COUNTDO
Y HIDING SOMETHING? 03:32 01:47 05:03 MAY LE
UNTDOWN BEGIN 09:06 10:33 11:45 RACE AGAINST
12 05:21 RACE AGAINST TIME RACE AGAINST TIME
UTH ... CONSPIRACY 365 TRUST NO ONE 06:07 SO
RIOUSLY MESSED UP HERE 08:30 12:01 05:07 06:4
O CAN CAL TRUST? SEEK THE TRUTH 12:05 MAY 0
CE AGAINST TIME 02:27 08:06 10:32 SEEK THE TR
7 SOMETHING IS SERIOUSLY MESSED UP HERE 0S
NSPIRACY 365 12:00 RACE AGAINST TIME 04:31 10
N CAL TRUST? 01:09 LET THE COUNTDOWN BEGIN
METHING? 03:32 01:47 05:03 MAY LET THE COUN
06 10:33 11:45 RACE AGAINST TIME 06:48 07:12 0
AINST TIME RACE AGAINST TIME SEEK THE TRUTH
S TRUST NO ONE SOMETHING IS 06:07 SERIOUSLY
RE 08:30 12:01 05:07 06:06 06:07 MAY WHO CAN T
EK THE TRUTH 12:05 MAY 06:04 10:08 RACE AGAIN
06 10:32 SEEK THE TRUTH 01:00 07:57 SOMETHIN
SSED UP HERE 05:01 09:53 CONSPIRACY 365 12:0
AINST TIME 04:31 10:17 MAY WHO CAN CAL TRUST?
UNTDOWN BEGIN MAY HIDING SOMETHING? 03:32
Y LET THE COUNTDOWN BEGIN 09:06 10:33 11:45
E 06:48 07:12 05:21 RACE AGAINST TIME RACE AG
EK THE TRUTH ... CONSPIRACY 365 TRUST NO ONE
06:07 SERIOUSLY MESSED UP HERE 08:30 12:01 0
07 MAY WHO CAN CAL TRUST? SEEK THE TRUTH
08 RACE AGAINST TIME 02:27 08:06 10:32 SEEK T
57 SOMETHING IS SERIOUSLY MESSED UP HERE